I0618403

In Full Uniform

Bo Starsky

Improbable
PRESS

First published by Improbable Press in 2021

Improbable Press is an imprint of:

Clan Destine Press
www.clandestinepress.com.au
PO Box 121, Bittern Victoria 3918 Australia

National Library of Australia Cataloguing-In-Publication data:

Bo Starsky
In Full Uniform

PB ISBN: 978-0-6489586-6-6
EB ISBN: 978-0-6489586-7-3

Cover artwork by © Willsin Rowe

Design & Typesetting by Improbable Press

Improbable Press
improbablepress.com

Thank you, Adam Driver, you magnificent beast,
for inspiring me to pick up my pen and start writing once more.

Contents

Letters from Fallujah

1

GROWING UP, HUAN ZHOU HAD ALWAYS HAD A CLEAR IMAGE OF WHAT he wanted his future to be like – a beautiful wife, two children, a big house, a good job, and one of those fancy Cadillacs Elvis used to drive. Because if there ever was a man to look up to, it was Elvis. And Ray Charles, but he couldn't drive on account of being blind so no vehicular aspirations resulted from his obsession with the coolest pianist to ever live. Back to the Cadillac and his future dreams: he was going to have it all, even if he was a skinny little twerp growing up on the poor side of New York where his immigrant mother struggled to keep them afloat.

The first part of that dream was abruptly changed when he was fourteen and realized he had a crush on his best friend, a boy. A boy who didn't like him back when it came down to it. He went from wanting a beautiful wife to having a handsome husband. Which didn't last very long when he found out such things were illegal.

Then came the reality of having to work for a living, that he couldn't just apply for any job he wanted and get it. He discovered weed in his later teen years and the rest unraveled from there.

Now he lives in a tiny little apartment in Washington D.C., because he followed a job opportunity that didn't work out. So here he is, working any job he can get his hands on, getting high in the evenings, and lamenting his lack of romantic prospects. Not to mention the fact that he still doesn't have a Cadillac, much less a driver's license.

Public transportation isn't that bad, after all, because it's on the bus that Huan meets Arthur.

Seeing young, twenty-something white men dressed in army fatigues and carrying a duffle bag isn't a rarity of itself, but there's something about this one that stands out. Not only is he broad in the shoulders with thighs that fill out those camo trousers perfectly, but he has the gentlest eyes of anyone Huan has ever seen.

He's in love.

Never shy about making the first move, Huan walks right up to him on the bus and says, "Is this seat taken?" He tries to be flirty with it, but on a scale of one to ten, where one is predatory and ten is Elvis' hips, he reckons he lands somewhere along three. Which is slightly weird and concerning but not giving off bad vibes. Then again, it's not as if he's very threatening to look at with his soft frame, slight pudge, and mismatched eyes.

His beautiful soldier looks up at him with his own mesmerizing eyes, and they hold the soul of a man just looking to be swept off his feet. He shakes his head one single time. Huan sits, smiling perhaps a tad too brightly. "I'm Huan," he offers, even though you don't usually offer your name to strangers on the bus.

The soldier turns his head to look at him again and Huan wants to guide him down to lay in his lap, run his fingers over that buzz cut and feel it prickle on his palm. Then with a solemn tone in a voice as soft and dark as his eyes he utters his name, "Arthur."

Jackpot!

He's in it now, there's a chance. The name on Arthur's fatigues reads as A. L. Hall, so Huan puts two and two together and figures on his name being Arthur Hall with a mysterious L in the middle he's not going to ask about. "How are you, it's a nice day, isn't it?" he asks instead, determined to take it slow this time and not scare off this prime cut of beef he's found entirely by accident.

"S'all right."

Huan nearly swoons on the spot. He's so stoic, and is that a drawl he detects?

"I'm just going into town for a slice of the cafe life," Huan reveals, "a nice cake and some sweet coffee to enjoy in the sun."

Arthur doesn't look like he's very interested in Huan's possibly pot-induced excursion to his favorite cafe downtown. "How about you? Coming home?"

"Nope, leaving." *Oh,* there goes that chance, his beautiful soldier from the south is being shipped out, it's a tragedy.

But perhaps not, he could still give it a shot and have a fleeting connection, maybe even more since it's not like Arthur isn't coming back. Right?

"Can I buy you a coffee?" For a few agonizing seconds he's afraid he's messed it up, but then something wonderful happens; a very slight smile creeps onto Arthur's plush, and very kissable, lips. It's a shy little thing that doesn't last for very long but it reaches Arthur's eyes and lights up his whole face.

"I'd like that," he says slowly, the twang in his accent perfectly paired with his dark chocolate voice.

Huan isn't nearly half as reserved with his own joy, beaming at the man sitting next to him, his date. Some part of him just knows this is the one.

They get off at his usual stop right down the street from the cafe, Huan feeling like a bit of bendy paper next to his clean cut soldier with good posture – who is also noticeably taller than him now that they're standing up. Everything about Arthur just keeps getting better and better.

Strolling down the street Huan deliberately walks closer to his beautiful soldier than he strictly needs to, their arms brushing together with little scratches of fabric. More and more this is turning into something out of a classic rom-com and he can't believe his luck.

Boldly taking Arthur's hand, Huan practically skips the rest of the way to the cafe, so happy he could sing. Their hands remain together the whole way, only separating when Arthur reaches to open the door for him like a true gentleman would. By the time they sit down Huan is already imagining trading heartfelt letters, and later a tearful reunion with his soldier at the airport where he'll be waiting with their dog and two children. Huan has no trouble entirely disregarding the amount of things they can get done in the short window of time they have together.

"What would you like?" Arthur's voice brings him out of his daydreams to rattle off his usual order and take out his card to pay before Arthur does that, too. Huan is the one who offered to buy coffee, after all.

Wanting some modicum of privacy for their date – that he suspects Arthur doesn't consider a date at all – Huan takes them to a corner table where they won't be surrounded on all sides by the morning commuters. However, the pause in conversation from the bus has brought them to a semi-awkward silence that he's determined not to let get in the way of his path to Prince Charming. Frantically he searches for something to say that isn't boring and run of the mill and comes up short.

"Where are you going?" he lands on at long last before immediately regretting it since he doesn't know if that's a rude question to ask or not.

Not missing a beat and oblivious to Huan's internal crisis Arthur takes a testing sip of his coffee and utters a single word. "Iraq." He takes another sip of his coffee. "It's my second tour, I don't know how long I'm gonna be there, usually about a year." So far in their short relationship that's the longest sentence Arthur has uttered, more words combined than he's said in the last half hour.

"I've never really been out of the country, unless you count the three years I lived in China after I was born," Huan says in lack of an intelligent reply. "Is it nice there? You know, away from the war zone?"

"It gets real warm, but it's real pretty too, where it ain't bombed all to hell, lotta good people. But I was right near the capital last time, I don't know how it'll be out in the countryside."

There's a look in Arthur's eyes that, months from now, Huan is going to understand in a different way. Today he only thinks the man looks a little sad which he can't blame him for; he has, after all, gone to war.

"You could tell me about it when you're there?" It's a bold

suggestion, but it's out now and he can only hope Arthur will turn him down gently instead of laughing in his face.

Arthur does neither of those things. He looks confused, then hopeful. "You want me to write you a letter?"

He wants to scream '*Yes please, write me many letters!*' An outburst he quickly shoves back down so he won't scare the love of his life away. "If you wanted to." A much more reserved answer and Huan gives himself a mental pat on the back.

The protests of *we've only just met*, and *I don't even know who you are*, never arrive. No, Arthur does something different that's so alarmingly cute Huan falls in love all over again. He smiles, ducking his head and bringing up one big hand to hide it behind, but one glimpse of slightly crooked teeth is all it takes to send Huan's heart fluttering like mad. "I'd like that."

"Really?" Huan voices his disbelief and stops picking at his pastry.

"Yup," Arthur says so quietly Huan almost misses it. "I ain't got a sweetheart to send anything to, just my brother that I ain't spoken to for a while."

There's something to be gleaned from that little tidbit if you listen just right, and Huan doesn't like what he's heard, but on the off chance he's wrong he's not going to voice that thought. For all he knows Arthur could have had a falling out with his brother over lots of things unrelated to his romantic persuasions. Though that doesn't change Huan's determination to make this man feel loved for as long as Arthur will let him. Huan's that kind of guy. All in. Always. Which *always* becomes a problem when guys think he's too much too fast and end up turning tail before too long.

As smitten as he is with the stranger across from him, he knows his bad luck in love is going to strike at some point, whether today or months down the line.

"Then I'll write you as many letters as you want, bombard you with them to make up for not getting any before," Huan grins, belatedly realizing his choice of words could have been better, but Arthur doesn't seem to mind. In fact, he seems to be an entirely different person to the broody soldier he'd met on the bus. "Here, let me give you my address." Before Arthur even has the time to open his mouth Huan has gone off in search of pen and paper.

One of the lovely girls behind the counter gives him a couple of pages out of her notepad and lends him a pen and he quickly jots down his address, email, and phone number. Arthur is still exactly where he left him, sitting there with his camo outfit and army green duffle.

For a moment Huan pauses to simply observe how he chews on his full bottom lip, the way he cradles his mug of coffee with both hands as if he's cold. But there's something so different about him from everyone else. He carries with him a certain gravitas despite his age, sitting there contemplating life like an old man. It's so charming and makes Huan wonder if he was attracted by the maturity, that maybe he wouldn't have noticed Arthur at all if he'd been slumping in his chair or leaning on the table like everyone else around him.

He stands out like a pillar of strength.

Huan slides the paper onto the table and retakes his seat. "I can't give you mine yet," Arthur says, "'cause I don't know if it'll change and I'll go someplace else yet, but I'll send you a letter soon as I get there to let you know." With meticulous care Arthur folds the piece of paper and Huan wonders what it'd be like to have those big hands on him, touching him so gently.

Then Arthur looks at the time, his wristwatch simple and scuffed from wear, the glass cracked on one side. "Shit, I got to go."

Huan's heart sinks, wishing this date could go on forever, but Arthur is already standing up and hefting his bag over a broad shoulder. In an effort to get as much out of this as he can Huan intends to walk his beautiful soldier back to the bus stop and wait with him.

So he does.

The moment they're back on the sidewalk Huan slips his hand back into Arthur's, feeling the calloused skin of Arthur's palm scratching against his own excessively moisturized one.

Back at the bus stop he feels like their brief time together is slipping through his fingers like sand, he's had his share and for all he knows there won't be any more, this could be it and he'll have to let Arthur go and never to see him again. The bus looms in the distance, drawing closer by the second, and Huan panics a little.

The lapels of Arthur's fatigues are stiff and starched as he grabs onto them, in stark contrast to how soft his lips are. He tastes like black coffee and Juicy Fruit gum, an odd combination that's hardly appealing, but the way Arthur leans into his kiss makes up for it in spades.

Then the hiss of a door opening breaks the moment and Huan has to watch Arthur climb aboard with a secret little smile on his face. He stands there by the curb until the bus is long out of view and the people have turned into passing wisps of color. "Goodbye, Arthur," he says, though it's far too late for it to be heard.

2

THE FIRST LETTER COMES AFTER THREE WEEKS OF HUAN PINING OVER a man he knew for less than two hours. The most wonderful man in the world; he'll argue with anyone who scoffs at his lovesick nature. He'd almost given up hope when there it was, a plain white envelope addressed to him in neat, heavy-handed print with a return address somewhere in Iraq. His heart beating in mighty thumps, Huan takes the letter upstairs, too excited to throw his junk mail into the bin by the mailboxes.

Kicking off his shoes by the door he hurries to his sofa, tearing the envelope open with trembling fingers and carefully unfolding the letter inside. On it is the same handwriting and he can't help comparing it to a typewriter, though more round in the edges.

Dear Huan,

They have put me in Fallujah this time, it's smaller than the town I spent my last tour at and farther away from the big city. They see more action out here, but I hope I won't get to see much. For the most part we just patrol and run drills waiting for something to happen. At least that's what my squad is doing, we're just the grunts so we don't get to know much. The other guys here are nice, I got a Sergeant here from West Virginia like me, though I have never met her before. She reminds me a little of my mother in how strict she is.

I have only been here a few days, but I keep thinking about you and the way you said goodbye. That was really nice. I have only ever been kissed twice before and both were girls, I didn't like it half as much as I liked kissing you. I hope you're having a nice time back there in Washington and going to that nice cafe with the good pastries.

I've never been much good at writing letters so I'm going to leave it here for now and hope you still want to send me one back.

Yours, Arthur

Huan can't keep the grin off his face, beaming brightly at the letter with its formal tone he can just about hear in Arthur's soft baritone and slow drawl. His heart beats wildly at the part about their kiss, overjoyed that he made any kind of lasting impression when he's hardly a master at the craft.

Not wanting to wait another second he rushes off to find the fancy stationary he'd bought for the occasion, the paper scented and faintly pink. It's the kind of thing that belongs in a romantic fairytale; it's perfect, not to mention feminine enough that Arthur won't be outed by it. He's heard stories about what happens to people like him and Arthur when they get outed in the military, and he'll do anything to avoid that.

Plonking back down on the couch he pulls the coffee table over with a screech of wooden legs on cheap floorboards, adding to the scuffs and scratches already there. "Right, then," he tells himself, pen in hand and blank paper before him. *What the fuck does he write back?*

Hi, Arthur,

Like you I'm not very good at writing letters, this is my first one since I was a kid and would write to my grandparents in China. It was my mother who did the writing, I just said what I wanted put down.

Washington is fine, it's been raining a lot this week so I haven't done much besides go to work and come back home, apart from last Saturday when I went to the bar down the street for a few drinks with the ladies that ended with me on the bathroom floor Sunday morning with my usual resolution never to drink again. I hope the weather is nice for you down there. Is it warm? I guess it is being in the Middle East and all. I've never been, I can't even remember much from before I came here to America. I was just three. Can you remember stuff from when you were three? I doubt it.

In other news, the corner store stopped selling my preferred brand of strawberry shampoo so now I have to find somewhere new to get it if I want to keep smelling like a summer day. And smelling good is important. I remember you smelled good whatever it was you were wearing that day, or maybe you just smell nice on your own. That would be nice. Imagine if I smelled like strawberries without having to use lotions and potions.

I'm glad you liked my kiss, I'm not much good at it either because a lot of guys say I come on too strong and we never get past the first date. I just want to do it right and not scare you off, but I couldn't just let you leave without knowing what it was like to kiss you. You tasted like black coffee and heaven. I hope you'll let me kiss you again when you come back.

XOXO

Your sweetheart, Huan

There, that'll have to do, right? Or maybe it's an awful letter and Arthur will hate it, everything from the pink paper and faint smell of strawberries to his god-awful handwriting. Maybe he should just write a new one? But then he'd be wasting the paper and the envelope he's already sealed and written the address on.

Gnawing on his lip Huan props it up against the fruit bowl that's never in use and leans his elbows on his knees to stare it down. He has to send something, but is this one good enough for Arthur? What if he writes a second one and compares them? No, that would only work if he had something else to say. If only he could write romantic sonnets like Shakespeare and wow Arthur with his mastery of words.

Alas, it is not to be, for he got a D in high school English.

Sighing, he leaves his seat on the couch to think about it. He could Google *how to compose a love letter of utmost quality* he supposes, but his computer is so slow and the internet connection patchier than a quilt so it would probably take hours. There's not much hope he can ever write something good enough for his Prince Charming.

It takes him two days to work up enough nerve to send the letter. Right after he's put it through the slot of the mailbox he wants to reach in and pull it back out. It's done now, he forces himself to move away and go back to work before his lunch break is over, for once. His boss is really starting to reach the limit of their patience and he'd rather not lose this job as well.

All he can do is hope and pray the letter isn't too much and scares Arthur away from sending another. He'd hate to ruin this too before it's even started.

3

A MONTH LATER HE GETS THE REASSURANCE HE NEEDS WHEN ANOTHER slightly bent envelope arrives in his mailbox, the same heavy hand on front. It's all he can do to not do a victory dance in the lobby of his building. He didn't scare Arthur away!

Racing up the stairs, he can't get home fast enough so he can sit down and read what Arthur thought was interesting enough to tell Huan about this time.

Being a little careless he manages to tear the envelope when he opens it, pulling out the folded paper that he can imagine Arthur sitting bent over with a pen in his huge hand, crooked teeth working over his bottom lip as he puts down the words.

Hello, Sweetheart

I hope this letter finds you well, we have had some trouble here since the last time I wrote but it was nothing big, just some gunfire and a mine went off, nobody was hurt worse than a scratch. It was lucky, I know of people who had it worse. In some ways I'm happy to be out here where we don't patrol the city as much so I don't have to see all the destruction from the bombs. Though sometimes my squad gets put in the nearby villages to help keep people safe when the enemy starts acting up nearby.

Really I don't like this at all, but someone has to do it and I figured I might as well since I was never much good at other things. I'm proud to be defending my country, I am, I just wish that it didn't have to be like this at all, that we could just stop this pointless fighting. If only the world did work like that. Being here is hard.

Sometimes they put on shows for us to make it easier. Stuff like singing and dancing and comedy. It's fun and easy, though they do it to distract us from what's going on. Without those shows this would be miserable. Just last week we had that Robin Williams come by to do a show. It was real good and he made sure to shake all of our hands after it was over and take a few pictures. He took one with my squad and we all got copies. I sent mine to you because I thought you would appreciate it more than my brother. He always liked Jay Leno better. I think Leno is all right, but Robin is better and I have never met Leno so he loses by default. Emmet would get mad if I said that. He gets mad about a lot of things, just like my daddy did before he died. He's a good man he just doesn't understand, he thinks it's a disease no matter what I say and I don't know how to make him listen.

I guess there are some things that will never change. I hope you have a good family that supports you, if not then I guess we're on the same train. I look forward to getting your letter, the pink was a nice touch and it smells like you too. Here we all smell like dirt and sweat so it was a nice change, and yes, it is warm, can get up to 120 at the worst, but it feels like twice that under all our gear. I'd like a little rain, that sounds nice.

Yours,
Arthur

Just like Arthur said there is a picture tucked into the fold of the letter that he's been too busy reading to look at. Picking it up from where it's fallen on the floor he looks it over, spotting Arthur in seconds. His beautiful soldier is a hard man to miss, standing tall almost a head above his squad with one of those careful smiles on his face, the kind that don't show off any teeth, and true to his word right in the middle of them stands Robin Williams. It's a fun picture that almost has a candid feel to it despite being posed. Huan is going to treasure it forever, get a frame and put it on display so he can proudly point at it and say, "That's Arthur, he's my boyfriend!" Even if his landlady is mostly the only one who sets foot inside his door. He should get some friends for the sole purpose of gushing about Arthur and his intention to live the American dream with him.

It's times like these he wishes his mother was still around, or that he'd had siblings. But going by Arthur's account of it, siblings aren't always what they're cracked up to be. Right now he wishes he could send hugs in the mail, make sure Arthur knows he's accepted for who he is and not sick in any way.

He should send a picture back. Question is how to do it without outing Arthur should anyone see it.

The solution is a little unorthodox, he'll admit, but hopefully it won't be any stranger than Arthur sending him a group photo.

Getting a disposable camera had been the easy part, it's a lot harder to find a group of girls who look approachable enough that he can ask them for a favor. He finds them at the coffee shop where he took Arthur, a group of women laughing over their coffees and cakes. They look so happy and carefree and Huan wishes he was part of something like that. But what really draws his attention the most is the slender brunette who looks like she could have been his sister in another life. If he can get a picture with them no one is going to question his being there.

Now he just has to do the hard part.

Luckily for him all his nail biting was for nothing once he's managed to explain the situation and awkwardly ask if they'll help him take a picture he can send his boyfriend in Iraq without outing him to his mates. Huan has never been one to rely on the kindness of strangers, but this has convinced him that maybe he should ask for help more often if it means he gets to take fun pictures with some lovely ladies.

They smile and fuss over his silly shirt with the bright polka dot pattern and gush over how nice it is of him that he's making an effort for his boyfriend. It's stupid, but for a moment he can pretend that they're his friends and they genuinely are out for a jaunt at the cafe to serve up some hot gossip while sipping their lattes.

Like everything else that illusion comes to an end when the pictures have been taken and he bids them goodbye, heading back out into the damp afternoon. He uses up the rest of the film taking pictures of dogs he meets on his way back to the shop to get his photos developed. In a few days he'll be able to send Arthur something to remember him by other than his messy handwriting with the big loops.

Two days later he has a little cardboard envelope containing a stack of twenty five pictures and a brand new frame for the one Arthur sent him. Now it's step three: choosing the right picture to send. He'll have to be strict with himself on this one or he'll end up sending them all, just in case.

It's not an easy choice, he loves them all, but the one he chooses has him and the brunette in the centre, so if anyone asks, Arthur can say, "My sweetheart is the one in the middle," and people will assume it's her.

If only it didn't have to be that way, if only he could just send a picture of himself and not have to worry.

Hello Sweetheart,

Thank you for the picture, I've framed it and put it up on the shelf with the one of my family so I can show you off when my landlady comes for the rent. I thought I should send you one back so I asked some lovely ladies for a hand and we took a few together so you wouldn't have to hide it if you wanted one. They thought it was a good idea even if I wish I could have done it without them. I didn't want to get you in trouble, I don't know how true they are but I've heard the stories about gays in the army.

But onto more positive things! I'm so jealous you got to meet Robin Williams, he's the coolest man alive! And I agree with you about Leno, your brother sounds like he's stubborn, I hope you can make him understand one day. My mom was great about me being gay, though she did cry about not getting any grandchildren. Even if I wanted any now she'd never have met them since she passed when I was 19. I'm sorry this got a little sad again. Must be the weather that's affecting me, (it's still a little grey and rainy over here). Do you get rain a lot in Iraq? I don't really know anything about it, I couldn't even point it out on a map if asked, all I know is that it's warm and dusty and that's from the bits they show on the news. Maybe I'll see you there if I keep watching? I bet you look hot in all your gear, maybe sexy would be a better word since you're probably dying from the heat so hot is a bit stupid. I can't even imagine what 120 is like, I hope you get plenty of water.

If I didn't think they'd melt I'd send you some chocolate. What is your favorite candy? I want to know those things about you, all your favorites.

Mine is Milk Duds and Kit Kats. My favorite color is pink, and I love sunflowers because they make me happy. You're my favorite person, outside of the ladies I get drunk with you're the only one I have and doesn't that just sound sad. And here I meant for this letter to be happier, full of rainbows and unicorns. If I could I'd draw you some but I'm afraid my artistic talents are lacking. Maybe I'll do it anyway and you can say it was drawn by a kid if it's really awful.

But now I should probably round this off so you won't have to read multiple pages of my rambling on about stuff that probably doesn't interest you. Please stay safe out there, you'd better come back in one piece so I can kiss you all over this time.

XOXO

Huan

Pleased with the outcome this time Huan doodles on the strip of blank paper left on the second page, trying his hardest to draw a decent unicorn for Arthur that ends up looking more like a deformed horse with a cancerous growth on its head. Huan thinks maybe the poor thing should be put down before it kills them.

For a moment he considers tearing that part off, but in the end he leaves it there thinking that Arthur might get a laugh out of it.

4

THEY CONTINUE THAT WAY FOR ANOTHER FEW MONTHS, TIME SLOWLY passing by as they learn about each other and Huan only falls more and more deeply in love with his beautiful soldier. The fact that Arthur hasn't gotten sick of him yet and claims to keep the picture of him in his pocket at all times warms his heart at night. He's spent many hours thinking about how a picture of him is so far away in another part of the world, living in the pocket of a soldier and offering him comfort when he needs it.

On his computer he's downloaded Skype because Arthur said that might be a possibility if he can get the time on the computer and figure out how. Huan really hopes he does so he can refresh his memory of that smooth baritone and drawling accent that pulls and stretches the words just right.

It's hardly been two weeks before Huan is roused from his pot-induced haze by a sound he's never heard before. Once he realizes what it is he's glad he only got in one hit from his bong. He races over to his computer and answers the call to find a grainy-looking Arthur staring back at him from a little too close to the screen.

A grin breaks out on Huan's face, so wide and bright it hurts his cheeks, but how could he not smile when his beautiful soldier is right there? Arthur looks much the same as he had the last time Huan saw him, only his close-cropped hair has grown a little longer, dark and warm in color. He's willing to bet it's soft if the way it's flopping just a little at the very ends is anything to go by. He hopes Arthur will grow it out further once he gets back.

"Hi, sweetheart." Arthur's voice comes out a little choppy, the connection leaving something to be desired, though Huan couldn't care less.

It's an effort but he manages to stop smiling like a loon long enough to utter a, "Hi, Arthur," back.

"You're looking good." When Arthur smiles at him Huan is

sure he's died and ascended to heaven right there. "I'm afraid I ain't got more than half an hour to talk to you on account of others needing to use the Skype as well, and since they got families they're the priority."

"Yeah, I can understand that, I'm guessing you said I was a friend?"

"Nope, I just didn't say you was a man, I'm alone in here so it ain't like anyone can see or hear you." As if to make his point, Arthur looks around, the image lagging a little when he moves too fast.

"That's good, then. Are they nice, your fellow soldiers? I still haven't gotten you in trouble?" That's always going to be a worry for him, his mind running away with scenarios where Arthur gets found out and the others beat him up or worse. Those are the most common ones, there's also the fear that Arthur will die and there's no one to tell him about it, that one day the letters just stop coming because his boyfriend was blown to bits.

He doesn't tell Arthur any of this, he'd hate to worry him.

"They're nice," Arthur nods thoughtfully, rubbing a hand over his five o'clock shadow. "And no, you ain't got me in trouble, I don't even know if there'd be much if they found out 'cause of the don't ask, don't tell. If they mighta found out about you being my sweetheart and all I ain't got to admit to nothing. They know a lotta the guys here give out a helping hand so it's not like they can fault me for having you when you're all the way over there and I still do my job here."

"Is that actually true? You give each other…" Huan makes a rude gesture, his face heating up when an image of Arthur participating floats into his mind on a little pink cloud.

"Some do, some don't. I've never cause I'm scared I might enjoy it too much, it's that kinda thing that might get me discharged, not carrying around a picture of you, no matter how pretty you are." The audio lags a little in places but to Huan that last part came in loud and clear: Arthur thinks he's pretty. "Even so, I don't cheat. We only kissed the one time, but I ain't about to go around behind your back."

How is he so perfect? Huan can't believe how lucky he's been, it would have taken as little as him choosing a different seat on the bus that day for him to have missed out on the stunning vision in camo that's now sitting six thousand miles away on the other side of the spotty connection.

"You all right there, Huan?" Arthur's question brings him back to the present and he wonders why he even asked about the handjobs anyway, but here they are.

"I'm fine, you just keep making me fall in love with you all the time. It's stupid, I know, cause we've only properly met once, but I really, really like you and I can't wait until you come back so I can hug you and take you out on a real date. I just want to treat you right." And here he goes, already on the edge of tears as Arthur stares dumbfounded at him from his computer screen, sitting so still the picture might as well have been frozen. Huan sniffles, waiting for Arthur to make his excuses about why this won't work after all.

"I only got about six months left over here then you can hug me all you like." Six months, that's so far away and so close at the same time. He can wait six months, then it'll have been a whole year since he met Arthur, since he kissed him at a bus stop in downtown D.C. A whole year of his life spent loving his beautiful soldier from all the way across an ocean.

Just six months until he gets to kiss those plush lips again.

5

THE NEXT LETTER HE GETS COMES WITH A POLAROID PICTURE AND A single square of wrapped nougat with a brand name printed in Arabic on the plastic. Huan unwraps it and takes a cautious bite, his mouth filling with a sweet nutty flavor that's absolutely divine. The picture is a candid one of just Arthur where he's sat on a chair cleaning his rifle. It's an unavoidable reminder of what his boyfriend does for a living and the danger he's in every day. Huan loves it anyway if only for the intense look of concentration on Arthur's face.

Hi, Sweetheart

We don't usually get a lot of sweets out here but sometimes we get supplies from the city and they will send us something to lift the spirits. I'm not much of a sweet tooth person, so I thought maybe you'd like it better since you like cake and all that. If you're allergic to nuts you'll just have to pass it on to someone who is not.

I really liked talking to you on the Skype, it was nice to see your face again even if it was all grainy and chipped, you are still just as pretty as that day you asked me out on the bus. You're the first one who ever did that, you know? Asked me out. When I grew up the boys were supposed to ask the girls but I was never interested in any of them, nice as they are. I don't think they were interested in me either, I was a weird looking kid. Now I'm going on my 23rd year and I finally met you who I guess I've been waiting for my whole life. Figures I'd meet you after signing away my own life to serve the country. That came about on account of me not wanting to become just another miner or farmer when my brother was set to make it big in baseball. He's been real bitter since he blew out his shoulder and even madder at me for not being around to look after our sick mama when I was on my first tour, she died before I got sent home so I missed the funeral too. Emmet never forgave me for that, I was just shy of 19. Then when he found out about me being queer he almost disowned me. Family isn't always all it's cracked up to be. I hope yours is better.

Things have been heating up a little over here, one of our patrols hit a road mine, you probably heard about it on the news, and there was a bombing a few towns over. It gets like this sometimes, then it goes quiet again and you know one of us is planning. I never want to know which one it is because I don't like being told to shoot at people, but I did sign up for this. At least that kind of thing doesn't happen that often, it's mostly explosives and missiles. I still sometimes regret signing up, it's scary being over here, and it doesn't get easier the second time around. I'm just as scared this time. Some nights I can't sleep because of how scared I am, and I wish I was back in America with you, but somebody has to do this to keep you safe. Can you imagine if no one ever joined the army?

Part of the reason why I'm so scared is that my family has a curse, bad things happen to all of us sooner or later and it's always something that ends up changing our lives by taking things away. I can't help thinking that the curse is going to come for me while I'm over here. Maybe I'll be the next guy to step on a mine or get taken prisoner. Any of that could happen tomorrow and it feels like it's more likely to happen to me over anyone else here. Emmet says it's all bullshit and that I'm superstitious about something that doesn't exist, but I have the proof as far back as I could get. We all had something happen to us.

Anyway, I'm sorry for bringing that up with you, I would have started a new letter, but I don't have any more pages in this notebook to write on and I don't want to ask for any from the other guys, they all have people to write to too. I only have five months to go now so I'll see you before you know it.

Yours,
Arthur

By the time he's reached the end Huan has chewed his way through the nougat and is smiling at this newly revealed aspect of Arthur's personality that he's obviously made an effort to hide. It's cute. And it's not like Huan can begrudge him his beliefs when he's superstitious himself. You won't catch him cutting his nails at night or growing a moustache, no sir.

Dear Arthur

Thank god you're superstitious, that makes me feel a lot better about crying when I knocked over my deodorant can and chipped the mirror. I couldn't figure out the math as to how much bad luck that was, but since I'm still alive I'm guessing you might have to break the whole thing to invoke the curse. I've been extra careful about what I keep around my mirror since then, I'm not risking seven years when I'm already pretty unlucky by the normal standards. I guess the worst that could happen is me losing you, every time I open one of these letters the pessimistic part of me thinks it's a Dear John. Would you believe me if I said this is the longest relationship I've ever had? People always think I'm weird and leave it at one date or less, I've only had one that got up to three. Not that you want to know any of this, I'm a habitual oversharer.

I really want this to work, please tell me if I'm being bad at it?

I know I always fall in love so fast and it scares people away, but I can't just not tell you how much you mean to me. I thought you were so gorgeous when I first saw you on that bus and when you opened your mouth I was hooked. I love how you talk. Your voice just fits you so perfectly, and that accent makes my knees weak. I can't wait to hear it in person again. Would you be offended if I told you I've gotten off to the thought of you saying dirty things to me?

XOXO

Huan

When Huan posts his latest letter he's brimming with anxious energy, sure that Arthur will be put off when he reads it and realizes how clingy he can be. It's a miracle that he's managed to keep from blurting all his feelings out before now.

Even when they were on Skype and on the subject of mutual masturbation he didn't say anything which must be a new record for him. He's impressed with his own show of restraint, heading back home to smoke and anxiously wait for the reply. That is if he hasn't made himself out as too much to deal with.

The worst thing about it is that he can't do anything but wait.

6

AND WAIT HE DOES, FOR ARTHUR'S NEXT LETTER, AND THE ONE AFTER that. The letters where they talk about desire and the secret thoughts they have about each other at night, the things they'd like to try. For each word Arthur has written to him, Huan thanks a God he doesn't believe in, amazed that his beautiful soldier is willing to share those things with him outright.

For weeks his mind is running amok with the things he could do with and to Arthur once he gets him into a bed. He'll spend hours getting to know what makes his boyfriend squirm and moan, track down all those little places to make him sing. They'll have to spend an entire week in bed when they're back together.

Then a few days shy of twelve months a letter arrives, one that has a good feeling to it from the second his fingers touch the yellow paper of the envelope. It's not a particularly thick one this time and it has no lumps or bumps to indicate any additional contents.

He takes the steps two at a time as he hurries up to his little apartment so he can read it in peace.

Hi, Sweetheart,

I have good news, I might arrive before this letter even gets to you so as you might have guessed they're sending us home. My tour is up and I'm still in one piece, imagine that. And soon I get to hug you, and kiss you, and do some of those things we talked about. I can't wait to see you again. I'm afraid I don't know yet the exact date and time of my arrival, but I know your address by heart so I'll come find you first thing after we land, all right? I'll be there before you know it.

Yours,

Arthur

As he reads the short letter an overwhelming sense of joy fills him. Arthur is coming home! This is one part of their future relationship they haven't broached yet; what happens next is a mystery for them to discover together.

He needs to clean.

He can't have Arthur staying in a dusty apartment littered with dirty laundry and smelling of weed. When was the last time he did a proper deep cleaning? Too fucking long, that's when. Scrambling up from the couch, he dives for the cupboard under the kitchen sink and pulls out his meager cleaning supplies to start right away. For all he knows Arthur could come knocking on his door any minute now.

Over the course of the next few hours he mops the floors, cleans the kitchen, and changes the sheets on his bed – they'll be dirty again soon enough but he's always preferred doing the horizontal tango in a clean bed. Nice sheets are just a bonus sensation; Huan doesn't have any of those, all his sets are worn and threadbare, bought at a fifty percent off sale. Maybe he should get some new ones? But that would require him to leave the building and he can't do that, what if Arthur arrives when he's out?

But Arthur doesn't arrive; not that day, or the next. By the third day Huan has started to think himself into a pit. What if Arthur isn't coming after all? Maybe he finally realized he doesn't want this at all once he set foot on American soil once more? Huan can't really blame him if that's the case. He wouldn't want to be attached to himself either.

He still doesn't stop cleaning, scouring the entire apartment from top to bottom, every cramped corner of it. All it does is make him wonder why he pays so much for a two-bedroom shoebox. The answer to that is because it's safer than anywhere he's lived before. He's grew up in worse places where drug deals took place at night and crime was a common part of people's lives, he'd rather pay out of his nose and live on ramen than go back to that.

He'd like it better if he wasn't lonely, though, and all he can do to combat that is hold onto that shred of hope that his beautiful soldier will come home. The hope that his letter just arrived earlier than expected and Arthur will be knocking on his door any day now.

When that day comes Huan is going to be ready with his clean apartment and the fancy packets of ramen so he can offer Arthur something to eat despite his lack of skill in the kitchen.

What he wasn't ready for was a phone call and a gruff voice greeting him with his own name attached to a question. "Is this Mr Zhou?"

Huan's gut drops like a lead balloon, mind racing through every awful thing that could have happened to Arthur; images of blood and gore flashing by. He's crying before he's even gasped out a weak yes, so sure that whoever this is is going to tell him that Arthur died weeks ago.

"My name is Major Callum, I'm calling on behalf of Arthur Hall who has named you as his emergency contact. There was an incident with the convoy he was travelling in to the airport, an IED by the side of the road." The Major sounds tired, voice worn down from years of making phone calls like these.

Huan sobs, sinking to his knees by the wall where his phone hangs. "Oh, God." He can't breathe, his body shaking too hard for him to get a proper breath.

"I can assure you Mr. Hall is alive and in good hands, he arrived at Walter Reed this morning and will be recovering here. You are more than welcome to come during visiting hours, I'm sure Mr. Hall will appreciate the support." Knowing that Arthur is still alive eases his fears somewhat, but he's still all alone in a hospital, probably in pain if he's awake at all.

"Now if you do come visit him you should be prepared to face the extent of his injuries. Would you like me to tell you or do you prefer not knowing?"

How could he ask a question like that? In what world would someone not want to know what has happened to their beloved? "I want to know, please. I want to know," he stutters, wiping snot and tears with the sleeve of his jumper.

Major Callum takes a breath, a rustle of papers coming through in the background. "Mr. Hall suffered extensive shrapnel damage and third degree burns to his left side, they were forced to perform a below the shoulder amputation at the field hospital."

In that moment Huan feels like he's the one who's been hit by a bomb, a piercing ringing in his ears drowning out everything else. His poor Arthur. He's known for a year that something like this might happen, that his boyfriend could get hurt, or worse – Arthur knew it too, but it doesn't make the news any easier to bear. He has to go see him, it wouldn't matter if he was still over in Iraq or right here in D.C., he has to go see him. This just isn't something he can let Arthur do on his own, especially not when he's the one who got the phone call and not Arthur's brother.

"Thank you for letting me know. When are the visiting hours?" God knows how long Arthur has been alone before they brought him here.

"Visiting hours are between 0900 hours and 1800 hours, there's a nearby hotel if you need accommodation. Would you like me to let Mr. Hall know you're coming?"

Would he?

"No, I want it to be a surprise." That way he could bring some flowers, maybe a cookie from the cafe where they had their first date. "Is there anything Arthur can't eat?" It doesn't hurt to be sure when it comes to this.

"Provided Mr. Hall wants to eat it, no," Major Callum chuckles, probably trying to lift the mood because he's tired of listening to Huan trying not to wail like a banshee.

"Thank you for calling," Huan mumbles around the lump in his throat, already looking at the clock and trying to estimate how long it'll take him to get to the hospital from here.

Really it wouldn't matter to him if there was only twenty minutes left of visiting hours, he'd still go and haunt the front door until someone lets him in long enough to just see that Arthur is alive and confirm what he's been told.

His trembling legs protest the move, but he can't sit here on the floor crying for Arthur when he can be right by his side. Shambling into the kitchen for his keys and wallet, he gets so far as putting them in his pocket before he realizes he's wearing pajamas and he doubts they'd let him in looking like this.

Dressing fashionably isn't exactly at the forefront of his mind when he yanks open the drawers on his dresser and pulls out whatever is closest no matter the color or pattern. As long as it isn't pajamas it's good enough for him and it had better be good enough for the hospital staff. And the city bus, they've seen way worse than a frazzled man in mismatched clothing crying in the back row.

After twenty minutes of equal parts pitying and annoyed looks he finally manages to stop sniffling and find the right bus, which he is currently not on but will find in two stops and a bit of waiting. If everything turns out right he should be seeing Arthur in less than an hour.

The time passes torturously slowly as he stares out the window. He finds his way from the bus stop to the gate of the hospital – which looks so much more ominous than any kind he's ever seen before. For one, he's never had to show his ID and be name-checked against a list by a military security guard that looks like he'd shoot Huan just as soon as let him in, his unemotional face looking like it's carved from rough stone.

But as terrifying as it is, he can't leave knowing Arthur is on the other side of that gate waiting for him to arrive, trusting him with his life should it, God forbid, ever get that far.

The guard lets him in, leaving him to walk through the compound following the directions he's given. He's reached the front door of what he hopes is the right building before he remembers he was supposed to bring Arthur something to eat. *Too late now*, he sighs, pushing into the quiet reception.

The lobby looks like any other hospital he's ever been in, though, the main difference being the mix of people in white coats and army fatigues. He feels like an idiot walking in looking like he does with his bad posture and awful clothes, though the nurse behind the desk still smiles at him when he approaches.

"How can I help you, sir?" she asks and her indifference to his appearance makes him feel a little bit better.

"I–I'm here to see Arthur Hall, my name is Huan Zhou." Even trying his best to sound confident Huan's voice comes out meek and rather like a question.

"Of course, do you need someone to show you to his room?"

Glancing around at the obvious military presence Huan doesn't need to be asked twice. "Yes, please?" He'd rather not wander around on his own in here.

Still smiling like there's nothing wrong in the world she waves over an orderly and instructs him to take Huan up to Arthur's room.

To Huan hospitals always have an underlying sense of dread attached to them, the knowledge that each room they pass by holds people who are dying or close to death. Knowing that Arthur is one of them and that he'll likely never be the same man Huan kissed at the bus stop that day one year ago. Knowing that being told the extent of his injuries is never going to prepare him for what he'll see with his own eyes. It changes nothing about how he feels, he still loves Arthur and he always will, only now they'll have to work harder.

When they stop outside a plain door with the number 8 on it Huan feels his stomach drop. The orderly, who has probably seen countless loved ones having to face the fear and heartbreak of such a reunion, gives him a pitying look. "Just hit the call button if you need anything and someone will be with you as soon as possible."

Huan can only nod, sure that if he opens his mouth no noise will come out of his parched throat.

The door handle is smooth and cold to the touch, yet seeming to burn all the same as he pushes it down, only remembering to knock when he's already opened it a crack. His voice trembles when he asks: "Arthur?"

It takes a few seconds and a rustle of sheets before there's an answer. "Huan?" And that's all it takes for the tears to spill over again, he sounds so small and tired, voice raw from screaming or crying – he doesn't want to know which, or if it's both.

Pushing the door open the rest of the way he searches out the figure in the bed, needing to see and confirm that it's actually Arthur and not some figment of his imagination talking back to him.

It's him all right, in the flesh, but even knowing about the amputation can't stop Huan from gasping at the sight of the bandaged stump that's the only thing left of Arthur's left arm. "Arthur," he whimpers, crossing the room to take up his right hand and clasp it between his own. Though the bruising is faded by now it still looks so painful where it creeps out from under bandages covering his left side, patches of skin turning green and yellow where it's not gnarled from burns. And that's only what he can see above the sheets at Arthur's waist.

Arthur's face is unscathed but the exhaustion is stark against his sun-tanned skin, dark circles marring his eyes, and sallow cheeks cutting him in sharp angles. "I can't look at it," he confesses with fear weighing down his words, "It feels like it's still there."

This isn't the same man Huan kissed goodbye all those months ago, and now that he's looking into Arthur's terrified eyes Huan thinks he might be in over his head. As scary as it is he can't just walk away, nor does he want to, because Arthur needs him, and he knows that he needs Arthur like a fish needs water.

What does he even say in a situation like this? How does he make it better?

He can't even imagine the place Arthur must be in right now, not to mention what he might want and need. The only thing Huan can do is his best – whatever that is.

Should he say sorry? That it's okay? Throw out empty promises that don't mean much in the grand scope of things? Because what he *can* imagine is that Arthur doesn't want to hear any of that when he's laying there with a boatload of fresh trauma and one less limb. To him things must seem impossibly bleak.

"I'm here," he says in the end, letting his left hand wander further up to stroke over the tanned skin of Arthur's forearm. "I'll look after you, Arthur, I promise." His skin is so cold and clammy under Huan's palm, the muscles quivering with the effort of holding back.

Arthur makes an aborted move with what's left of his left arm, face turning pale from the pain and his eyes turning wet with the reminder. When the first tear spills over Huan wipes it away. The floodgates open and more follow, and even though he's scared of hurting his beautiful soldier, Huan sits on the edge of the bed and tries to maneuver him into a comforting embrace.

It's awkward, but Arthur doesn't seem to mind, clinging to him while heaving sobs wrack his body. Listening hurts; Huan's own face is wet with tears while Arthur makes the most heart wrenching sounds he's ever heard.

Huan realizes, while he sits there stroking over Arthur's overgrown buzzcut, that while he's really not who should be doing this, Arthur doesn't have anyone else. His brother is clearly not interested, or unwanted, since Arthur had them contact Huan over his own family, and as far as Huan knows there is no one else. *He really is all Arthur has.*

Arthur cries for a long time, broken sobbing turning into hitched breathing turning into eventual silence. A heavy kind of silence that lays like a thick fog over the room, filling their lungs and making each breath a challenge of its own. Neither of them know the right thing to say or do, where to go next from here. Ahead of them lies a maze with no map and any number of traps and pitfalls. The best they can do is take it one step at a time.

The remaining two hours they spend in near silence, Arthur clinging to him like he is the last drop of water in a desert. It physically hurts Huan to leave Arthur there all alone.

Tomorrow morning he'll be here at 9 o'clock sharp.

And he is, going through the same procedure as yesterday at the gate then finding his way to Arthur's room with a bag of freshly baked muffins from a bakery by the bus stop. They'd smelled delectable the whole way here, giving him hope that maybe he could tempt his boyfriend to have a bite.

When he quietly opens the door and finds Arthur asleep Huan smiles, thinking he looks so peaceful that way despite the bandages and bruising. His immediate thought is that he wants to kiss him; Arthur's lips look so soft and inviting, slightly parted and red from being chewed on. He settles for pressing a barely-there kiss to Arthur's temple instead, not wanting to disturb him when he's finally getting some rest.

Putting aside the muffins he takes up the visitor's chair, sitting back to watch Arthur sleep and listen to the ambient noises of the hospital. He finds it almost peaceful despite knowing that all around them are injured soldiers in various states of health carrying with them trauma from a country he's only ever seen on CNN.

Religious or not, Huan still bows his head and sends out a prayer for everyone in this hospital and the soldiers still out there, and a thank you for getting his Arthur back alive.

Movement catches his eye and he looks up to see Arthur's face twisting in something like fear, his calm replaced by a furrowed brow as he mumbles in his sleep. *Please let it pass,* he thinks, anyone can see plain as day that Arthur needs every hour of sleep he can get.

It doesn't pass.

It gets worse.

Arthur writhes in the bed, combating demons disguised as bedsheets. What does Huan even do in a situation like this? Even after spending most of the night on Google looking up ways to help with trauma, amputation, and PTSD he can't for the life of him remember any of it now that he's watching Arthur have a nightmare. Is he supposed to wake him or not? Should he try to soothe him? Maybe he shouldn't do anything at all. But the part of him that loves Arthur overrules the logical part, and he carefully lays a hand on a muscular shoulder and shushes him softly in an attempt at lulling him back to sleep.

It doesn't work. Arthur jerks away from his touch and wakes with a broken scream when he rolls onto the stump of his left arm. When he opens his eyes they're glassy and distant, right hand clutching at something that's no longer there, forcing Huan to watch the horror of realization come over Arthur's face.

"Arthur, darling?" Huan slowly reaches for him and lays a hand on his rapidly rising and falling chest. "Try to breathe. I'm right here with you, you're safe." It feels futile to say things like that but what else is there? If he could wave a magic wand and fix it all, he would, but this is the real world and any magic that exists he's going to have to work hard for.

"It hurts," Arthur whimpers, his voice so unnaturally small for a man his size.

Unsure if the pain is physical, mental, or both, and unwilling to take that chance, Huan pulls the little string with a red plastic tip. A nurse shows up within minutes, breaching the little bubble Huan has been building in his mind to hide from reality just for a little while.

She does a quick assessment of the scene before stepping back out of the room. Huan wants to demand she come back and do something, forgetting in his fear that the nurses aren't a walking pharmacy. Coming back with a bit more rush in her step she injects something into the cannula in the crook of Arthur's arm, not batting an eyelash at their entwined hands. In just a few seconds some of the tension is released from Arthur's body while the nurse examines the now bloodstained bandages.

"We'll have to change these, Mr. Hall," she says matter-of-factly. "If your friend would maybe go get a cup of coffee in the cafeteria?"

Huan has barely enough time for his brain to even suggest a faint smile and nod before Arthur's grip on his hand tightens. "No, I want him to stay." His tone is firm despite the lingering tremble from being woken in such a painful way, and squeamish as he is Huan isn't about to deny him a single thing. He'll need to learn how to do this anyway if he's to be looking after Arthur when he's released.

The nurse looks like she's about to protest but after taking one look at the white-knuckled grip Arthur has on him, she relents with a sigh. "Are you sure you're all right with this?" she asks Huan.

He nods. All he can do in this situation is just bite the bullet and get it over with.

"I'll be back in a minute with the supplies."

Watching her leave he's taken by surprise when Arthur speaks again. "I'm sorry you got to see this."

"It's all right, I need to learn how if I'm going to help you. I'm not leaving you over this, Arthur." It's plenty obvious that they've both already had that thought but come to different conclusions. "I was so happy when I got your letter, I couldn't wait to see you again." He wishes it could have happened in a different setting than this but what matters the most is that his beautiful soldier came back to him, even after a year of being exposed to his eccentricities.

"I didn't know what to do, I couldn't have them tell Emmet but I shoulda asked before changing you to my contact."

"It's fine, I'm glad you did. I don't want to judge but your brother doesn't sound like the most caring person." If it stood between him and Arthur's brother he'd want to take responsibility every time because at least that way he'd know Arthur was getting the support he needs in a healthy way.

"Emmet's got his opinions and they don't always line up with everyone else's." There's a desolate look in Arthur's eyes when he speaks and Huan wants nothing more than to hold him, but before he can the nurse comes back carrying a metal tray loaded with bandages and disinfectants.

Watching her change the dressings really brings to light just how lucky Arthur was to survive; if it had been Huan laying in that bed he knows he'd be crying all the time. The burns take up so much of his left side, almost from shoulder to waist and he can't even imagine how much it must hurt though the nurse assures him it looks healthy.

Dealing with the amputation is hardest of all, it just really puts it in perspective that part of Arthur is gone forever. For some reason he'd expected it to look worse and not be a neatly stitched cross that the nurse has him carefully clean with a cotton swab. Touching it is strange, but he's relieved that it does nothing to lessen his feelings for Arthur, it's just another aspect of the man that he loves.

7

THE NIGHTS ARE THE WORST. AT FIRST ARTHUR HAD BEEN TOO NUMB and shocked to feel much of anything about anything, drugged up in a hospital bed in Iraq. Then they moved him back Stateside, loaded him on a plane with a bunch of others that were also too injured to be of any use to the army. He'd felt numb and empty up until the moment Huan walked into his room with red eyes and a splotchy face. Then he'd felt guilty for naming him as his emergency contact, for putting something like this on his shoulders when they barely know each other even a year down the line. But Huan had taken one look at him, walked across the room, and taken his callused hand in his smooth ones.

It had felt good. And Huan had let him cry in his arms so he could let off all that pain he'd been carrying with him since they pulled him out of that burning wreck and saved his life.

Then it had been night again; Arthur left to the demons in his mind while the world slept peacefully around him. Every single night since he first woke up with one arm less has been painful, his mind replaying the horrors he's seen on repeat until he wakes screaming himself raw. That's when he wishes Huan was here the most.

But the rules dictate he can only be here during the visiting hours, and he has been for the last three days, from nine in the morning to six in the evening he's there, waiting patiently outside when the doctor comes by, and learning everything he needs to know when the opportunity arises. They haven't talked about what's going to happen when they finally release him. Arthur can't find the energy to bring it up, but it's plain to see Huan is getting ready to welcome him into his home where he's somehow expected to recover from what he's been through.

It's not that it's impossible, he's seen people do it before; what scares him is his own doubt in his ability to get through it. Part of him wishes he'd just died in the explosion so he wouldn't have to live with the aftermath.

He's just glad he doesn't have to do this on his own.

Without Huan he'd have his brother, and though he loves Emmet, he's difficult and set in his ways. They were both raised on the Bible, only Arthur stopped believing after his first tour. No benevolent God would ever let something like that happen, the things he's seen, it hurts him to think about it.

Signing up had been his way of getting out and making something of himself; at eighteen he'd been fresh-faced and naive, desperate to get away from his small town roots and grow into a man free from his family's old-fashioned views. Then he'd met a strange man on the bus and fallen head over heels for him by the time he kissed him goodbye at the bus stop two hours later.

His relationship with Huan is the first thing Arthur has had that's for him and him alone, each letter helping him hang on while living life in a war zone. After their talk on the Skype he'd changed his emergency contact because he knew then that if something was to happen to him Emmet wouldn't respect his wishes. And he knew that if he got hurt and needed help he wouldn't be able to recover with Emmet preaching about his sins and blaming it all on Arthur being *wrong*.

However, Huan, his sweetheart, the man who says he loves him, doesn't deserve the burden of looking after him, either. It doesn't feel right putting this on him and Arthur would prefer it if he didn't have to, but Huan is all he has left.

Getting back on his feet won't be easy, he'll just have to trust that he'll be able to pay Huan back someday for everything he's sacrificing.

It's his fifth day back in the States. His boyfriend arrives like clockwork and takes his hand, leaning in to press a kiss to his forehead since the room is empty and there's no one around to see them for what they are. Being discharged is inevitable, now that he's useless to the army, still he'd prefer it not to be a dishonorable one for just being a certain way. Coming to terms with that took him a long time and he's not about to let it screw him over again.

"Good morning, I brought you some strawberry scones today." Huan smiles and Arthur falls a little bit more in love, amazed that he'd been lucky enough to have this in the middle of everything else.

For Huan's sake he forces a smile and it almost feels natural. "Thank you, sweetheart." Maybe if he keeps smiling it'll feel like it's supposed to? He'll just have to keep trying because giving up isn't an option.

A sharp stab of pain goes along his left arm that isn't there, making him flinch and instinctively reach for it before remembering. "Do you need me to call the nurse?" Huan asks quietly, looking up from the bag of scones.

"No, I'm fine." It'll hurt anyway, besides, he can't depend on painkillers his whole life just because his body is confused. At least he himself has gotten over the initial shock of waking up with one arm less, now he has to learn to live with that.

Which is easier said than done.

"Let's go for a walk," he suggests a few hours later, well after they've eaten their scones and the doctor has been by to check on his progress. After days spent confined in one hospital room or another he's desperate to get outside and feel the air on his face.

It's slow going, but they make it, and outside of Huan's soft kisses it's the best thing he's ever felt. Compared to where he grew up, D.C. is loud; even on the closed-in campus of the hospital the sounds of traffic are easy to hear, but after being in a war zone for a year it's the most beautiful sound he's heard. Not a single gunshot or explosion, no crying, arguing, or screaming. He pities the people of Iraq that have to live with that. No one should have to live with that.

They sit on a bench to take a break when the burns in his side start to pull and hurt too much. How Huan can stand to look at it when they change the bandages Arthur doesn't understand, he can't even look at it himself. Every time he turns his head and sees the nothing and the bandages he wants to cry.

Who's to say Huan doesn't feel the same way? Maybe it all just comes down to his boyfriend being stronger than him. And isn't that what he needs right now?

Letting his head loll onto his right shoulder Arthur watches Huan next to him, the way his eyes scrunch up against the sun, one grey and one brown, and his dark, unruly hair moving in the breeze. Those unique eyes turn to lock onto his and the scrunch turns into a smile. This time when Arthur smiles back he can't find anything wrong with it. "I love you, too," he says while he still has that feeling in his chest, finally replying to what Huan confessed what feels like ages ago.

He watches the smile brighten and those beautiful eyes turn a little wet around the edges. "Really?" Disbelief colors his voice, a warm hand clasping his own.

"Really." A quick glance around shows that they're alone in this moment so Arthur quickly presses a kiss to Huan's lips to prove it.

"No one's ever said that to me before."

In that moment Arthur knows it'll be okay because the way Huan looks at him is the light at the end of the tunnel. That wide-eyed warm look of surprise and unconditional love. When he woke up back in Iraq he'd thought there was no way Huan would ever look at him with anything other than horror and disgust when he saw what was left of him, but he just had to be amazing and prove him wrong.

"Then they were all dumber than a box of rocks." How could anyone not fall in love with Huan when everything about him is so lovable? To Arthur he's perfect all the way from his unruly hair to the softness around his middle and the colorful way he dresses.

Huan makes a noise somewhere between a sob and a laugh that comes out a bit wet sounding. "I can't believe I found you on a *bus.*"

"I'm glad you found me on that bus cause I was scared back then." Like he is now but for different reasons. When he got on that bus he didn't have much to lose anymore, his relationship with Emmet so strained it's almost hostile, then Huan came up to him just like that and he suddenly had hope for something better, something to come back to. Now he's scared of so much more than just dying; of things that are worse than dying. "You were like my own personal angel." Superstitious as it may be, Arthur is sure that carrying that picture of Huan in his pocket is what let him survive something he shouldn't have, and as torn as he is between wanting to have died and needing to see his sweetheart again, he just has to have faith that the God he doesn't believe in made the right choice for him.

Arthur uses the sleeve of his hospital pajamas to wipe Huan's teary face for him, whispering soothing words and hoping he's doing it right. Comforting others has never been something he's been good at when all his life he's been told – either by men in his family or men in uniform – not to show emotions, to just suck it up when something hurts him and not ask for physical comfort. When it comes to Huan all of that can go out the window and into the landfill where it ought to be.

"It's all right, sweetheart," he hums, using his arm to tuck Huan against his side where he can cry on his shoulder. Right now he couldn't care less if anyone sees them and reports it, honorable or not doesn't matter so much when his boyfriend needs him.

Bawling is a better word for what Huan is doing as he clings to Arthur like a little bramble, it's intensely emotional and he loves every second of it simply because it's the most positive thing he's ever experienced. Now, he's not about to claim his family never loved him or any such thing, but this is different, this is his and entirely unfounded in anything like being related; Huan simply loves him for being him.

He loses track of how long they sit there on that bench holding each other and crying, Arthur in so much awe of how careful Huan is being with him, yet not shying away from any of his injuries. He's simply very, *very* careful about how lightly he rests his hand on Arthur's waist right about where the bandages come to an end. Past his mother he can't remember anyone ever being that gentle with him. If anything it lets him know that it was fate who put them on the same bus that day.

Maybe there is a higher power after all, one that sent him his very own guardian angel.

When they pull back from the hug Huan's face is wet and

blotchy, but there's a smile on his face ten miles wide. It lets Arthur know that, even if things are difficult right now, he's never going to be alone.

8

COMING BACK TO HIS ROOM IS A MISERABLE REMINDER OF JUST HOW long the road ahead is yet, filled with endless hours of therapy and check-ups. They're not even going to start him on prosthetics until next week when the bandages can come off. Arthur isn't looking forward to that part because it'll force him to acknowledge the part of him he can barely even look at. Although getting a prosthetic will, at least, give him the ability to look more normal when he has to reintegrate to civilian life.

He's just barely gotten his singed carcass back into bed, staying clear of his sore side, and received a kiss for the effort, when there's a knock on the door. Before he's gotten out so much as a peep it swings open and a twist of criss-crossing emotions clench in his gut. Right there in the doorway with his bootcut jeans and worn out t-shirt stands his brother, a mighty scowl on his handsome face and a furrow in his brow.

"Arthur Leonard Hall, you mean to tell me your ass has been back home for a week and I only get to hear about it through the god-danged mail? I thought I was your next of kin?" Twisting his trucker cap between his weathered hands he steps into the room, finally casting a look at Huan. It's not a very kind one. "And who's this chucklefuck?"

Looking between his boyfriend and his brother, Arthur frowns, his good mood gone in a flash. "Don't you think that if I'd've wanted to see you right now I'd've let you know?" Working his bottom lip he takes Huan's hand in his, silently telling him to stay put because he's not sure he could deal with Emmet alone when he's feeling as fragile as he is.

"Arthur, we've talked about this." Emmet gives their hands a sour look. "You ain't got to be like this, we can get you fixed."

Huan's grip on him tightens significantly as he turns a deadly glare on Emmet, Arthur would hate to be in his place right now.

"If anyone needs to be fixed, it's you."

The brother in Arthur wants to halt what's on its way to becoming an argument, but the part of him that's a man in love thinks that maybe he should let his boyfriend stand up for him. His boyfriend that looks about as dangerous as a kitten, whereas his brother is about as broad as a barn, though shorter than both of them. Emmet is a brawler – an ex-baseball player that had a promising future taken away by a shoulder injury that pulled a college education out from under him in the process – and Arthur has no doubts who would win in a fight. The bigger question is if Emmet is going to let his hatred get to him in a military compound where even the nurses know how to flatten a man if need be.

"Who you talking to, chink? Why don't you go home?" Emmet squares up, crossing his arms and taking a step closer until Arthur is the only thing keeping them apart with his burnt and broken body.

"If Arthur wanted you here he would have told them to call you," Huan bites back with terrifying coldness.

"Arthur is *my* brother, and you ain't got no business filling his head with that queer crap."

"That *queer crap* is who he is and if you can't accept that he has every right to cut you out."

"Oh, so you're his mama now, is that it?"

"STOP IT!" That's enough, he's not going to just lay here and listen to them arguing about him and for him like he's not even here. He should have a say in his own damn life.

Both of them are looking at him with eyes like saucers; it's not often he raises his voice and he knows that to each of them it means different things. Huan has seen him hurt and crying, needing comfort and support more than anything; has listened to his fears and confessions that he's never dared tell anyone. Emmet, on the other hand, has seen him angry and spiteful, looking for glory and a way to escape so he wouldn't be the lesser Hall. So when he shouts to one of them he's angry, and to the other he's hurt.

Neither of them are wrong.

"Huan's right, Emmet. It's like I been saying for years. I love him and I ain't gonna let you try to break that just cause you want me to be miserable too." He's already had enough misery for a lifetime.

Emmet sighs, softening for a moment. "I don't want you to be miserable, Arthur, which is why you gotta see that this is unnatural. God didn't make you to be like this."

Huan squeezes his hand in silent support, looking a little embarrassed about his earlier outburst. "God said to love everyone, maybe you need to read the Bible again," he says with a soft smile, not so much as glancing in Emmet's direction.

"There ain't anything decent about what y'all are doing, it'll lead you right down to hell."

Now, Arthur can't pretend that Emmet's words don't sting, because that's just not true, it's just that from years of hearing the same speech it's more of a dull, familiar pain. Sort of like picking on a scab. What makes it hurt even more right now is that his own brother can't look past his bigotry and see the bigger picture. And if Arthur believed in heaven and hell he's pretty sure he'd be going downstairs for things a lot worse than being gay; like the few times he's shot to kill, or stood by and watched someone else do it.

War changes people and it's rarely for the best.

"I want you to leave now." Emmet looks at him like he's gone funny in the head, and maybe he has. "If all you're gonna do is talk bad about me and my boyfriend I want you to leave."

"Arthur…"

"I'm not gonna budge on this. You can come back tomorrow if you got something nice to say instead of preaching. If you don't, then I reckon you oughta just head back home and forget about me."

Emmet sighs, uncrossing his arms to put his hands on his hips. "Arthur, don't be like that."

On his other side Huan is standing in silence, mismatched eyes locked in a defensive glare, and as much as Arthur doesn't want anyone to be fighting over him it warms him to know that his boyfriend refuses to back down while still respecting Arthur's choices.

Unlike Emmet, who seems to only consider his own wants and needs, looking no further than the pages of his Bible and the attitude of the generation before them.

"Don't be like what? Himself?" Huan snaps.

Emmet opens his mouth to bite back and Arthur figures this is when the quotations come in, but then he pauses, closes his mouth, turns around, and walks out. He must have taken the defeat for what it is, two against one is never good odds. Arthur never thought he'd see the day. Still, there's a part of him that wants his brother to come back here tomorrow and say what he's always wanted to hear from him.

That's one thing Arthur knows isn't going to happen, not for a long time, maybe not even a lifetime and that hurts just as bad as anything else right now.

However, he's not alone in this room so he can't just sit here and mope.

"I didn't mean to drag you into all this," he tells Huan, giving his clammy hand a squeeze. *But god damn it if he isn't grateful he didn't have to do it on his own.*

"Are you okay?" Huan asks back, completely ignoring Arthur's apology.

"I don't know." And that's the honest truth. While he's too tired to feel right now, something like this is going to hit like a bag of bricks once it sinks in that this might have been the last time he ever saw his brother. That's the kind of thing that'll haunt a man every time it comes to mind.

"I'm sorry for yelling, but I couldn't just let him talk like that." Seating himself on the edge of the bed, Huan cups Arthur's jaw with his free hand, his touch warm and gentle, a soft thumb stroking over his cheekbone. It makes him feel like the long slope of his jaw was made to fit in the cradle of Huan's palm.

"And I can't blame you for getting mad." He's wanted to yell at Emmet plenty of times himself; has, too, on a few occasions, but it's always been a losing fight when he's been on his own. "I don't want to see him go, seeing as he's the only family I got left. Mean as he is."

"Maybe he'll change," Huan says and it's clear he's forcing a measure of hope for Arthur's sake.

"Maybe." But he doubts it.

9

Emmet doesn't come back the next day, or the day after that.

The world keeps turning despite the dark abyss he's dangling over in his mind, sorely tempted to look down and lose his grip on the rocky slope of his recovery. Up above him Huan is calling his name, reaching out for him and waiting patiently until Arthur can catch up and take his hand. His brother might have done the same if Arthur had been willing to make a promise that would only have caused him more pain.

It's unfair that it's like this, that the last of his family can't see beyond a thing so stupid as who he falls in love with and who he doesn't. Why should it matter at all?

Now all he has is Huan, and a horde of overworked medical staff trying to fit him for a prosthetic he's not sure if he wants. On one side of the coin he'll get a way to cover up the scarred lump that remains of his arm, on the other it'll be a constant reminder of what he'll never have again. It's barely been two weeks since he woke up without it and he can still feel it there, itching to reach out and touch, and failing to do so when he tries. Then there's the pain, the stabbing, burning pain that keeps him awake at night wishing he'd just died with the others.

What kind of life is a life full of pain and loss. Then he thinks about Huan who comes to see him every day from all the way across town. He's there the second they allow visitors all the way until the nurse comes to send him on his way. It makes him wonder what his boyfriend is sacrificing to be here with him, putting his entire life on hold like that to look after him and hold his hand.

Not to mention the way he looks at him like nothing has changed between now and one year ago, like he isn't scarred and broken, scruffy and unkempt. Huan still kisses him the same way too, like it never stops feeling like the first time.

How lucky he is to have that.

They'll be discharging him soon, sending him off into the world to deal with his own problems once their generosity on therapy runs out and the bills get that much bigger. Arthur's not sure how he's going to pay for it all because he won't let that lay on Huan. He has his combat pay and his pension but that can only reach so far.

Soon enough he's going to have to find himself a job and figure out the rest of his living situation since he's not expecting Huan to take him in and he doubts Emmet would accept him back now. He's not even sure if he wants to go back home to West Virginia now that the only things for him there are his memories of growing up scared, confused, and hating himself for something out of his control.

Until the day he met Huan he'd never even kissed anyone in public before, much less a man. It had come as a surprise that he'd felt so good about it as he had. Moving on from it would have been easy, he could have thrown away the note with Huan's address on it and that would have been that, they'd never have seen each other again. But as he was getting on that bus to the airport he'd known this was going to change his life; he was in love with that cute boy smelling like strawberries long before the thought ever occurred to him. There was no way he wouldn't send that letter.

And right now that boy is waiting in a chair, smiling encouragingly as the doctor fits a prosthetic over Arthur's shoulder and fastens the strap over his chest. It's tight and it pulls uncomfortably, pinching the skin below his armpit. Getting used to this isn't going to be any easier than everything else he's been through. But when he looks at that glowing smile things don't seem as bad as they once did. It's even distracting enough that he misses what the doctor says.

He shakes off his stupor, looking away from Huan whose eyes twinkle knowingly. "What?"

"How does that feel?" she asks again. The badge on her white coat reads Dr. Ortega and Arthur feels a little embarrassed for having missed it for so long. He's been in with her three times now, even been introduced, and still her name managed to slip by him.

"Kinda pinchy right here." Forgetting himself for a second he goes to point with his left hand, the movement pulling on the prosthetic's wire and bending the arm. He sighs, not sure he'll ever stop thinking his arm is there and getting a slap in the face from reality.

Dr. Ortega's face softens and Arthur figures his must have done something to betray the blip of distress. "I'm sure it's not what you want to hear, but it'll get easier, I promise." She pats him on the shoulder, moving to adjust the strap under his arm. "Is that better?"

Arthur wants to hate her for her pity, angry at himself for not having adjusted by now; yet he can't. He's never been a hateful man and getting angry at a doctor for doing her job isn't fair of him. "Yup," he sighs, letting go of that bubbling anger and frustration.

"I think it suits you," Huan pipes up from his seat and it does help knowing his boyfriend doesn't think less of him for being part plastic.

"It doesn't make you any less handsome, that's for sure." Hearing that makes Arthur sure that Dr. Ortega knows exactly the kind of relationship they have, and as nervous as that makes him, she doesn't seem to mind, treating him no different than she did before.

In three days they're letting him go, sending him off with a plastic arm, his dog tags, and a set of fatigues since all of his burned up in the wreck. Arthur can't wait to leave this place, but at the same time he's scared because it means he'll be leaving behind the life he's lived since he was eighteen years old. His entire life that burned up in a wrecked Humvee down in Iraq, even that picture of Huan he'd been carrying for good luck, his vest abandoned in favor of making him easier to move.

Now that he's sitting here mindlessly doing as he's told to operate the basic prosthetic, all he wants to do is cry and he's not even sure about what. Everything, he reckons.

There isn't much worth *not* crying about these days.

Across the room Huan is looking at him as if he knows what Arthur is feeling, that he's tired of holding it together in front of everyone. Still he can't just do something like that and make a spectacle of himself. He doesn't want to be seen as any more of a sissy than he already is.

It feels like the session is never ending, dragging on through endless repetitions until Arthur feels like he's made of glass and will shatter at the slightest push. Somehow, against all odds, he manages to keep it together until they're back in his room; the click of the door closing behind him acts as a trigger. Before he knows it tears are spilling over and leaving warm trails on his cheeks that Huan quietly wipes away for him.

His breath hitches and the dam is broken, Arthur sinking to his knees right where he stands. Huan goes with him, holding him close and whispering soothing words he doesn't understand.

As much as it hurts, it feels good to let it all out, he hasn't cried like this since the first day Huan came to visit him and though it hasn't been long it feels like years, time dragged to a sticky crawl designed to make him feel the pain of his own fractured mind. He fears a future where every day is going to be this difficult and eventually drag him down into the ground for good. That he'll try to drink it away and only make things worse. That he'll become angry and bitter and take it out on Huan.

He wants so desperately for none of that to happen.

And there comes the fear of knowing he's the only one who can keep it away. He won't be able to do it on his own, but in the end he's the one who makes the choice. All he can do is hope he doesn't drag anyone down with him if he can't get back up.

Arthur loses track of how long they sit on the floor like that, his sobs calming into eventual silence. It leaves him feeling raw and empty, like he's been rinsed on the inside, the tears taking with them a good deal of the weight on his shoulders. Everything seems a little less bleak now, hope breaking through the clouds.

Huan stays with him the whole time, stroking his unkempt hair and kissing his forehead, giving him all the time in the world to gather himself.

10

It's funny being back on the bus where everything started; only this time Huan is right next to him the entire time, holding his hand even though it's plastic. No one around them even looks up, too caught up in their books and magazines or talking on their cellphones to notice an odd couple sitting near the back. D.C. looks much the same as he remembers it, grey and full of concrete; it's not a place he'd ever have chosen for himself. But it has a bright spot that makes it worth sacrificing nature and farm land.

After a while they get off to wait for their next bus, and a bakery immediately draws his eye, the logo on the glass familiar. Huan must have noticed him looking; he asks, "Do you want to see if they have more of those muffins you liked?"

He would, just not like this, he's barely presentable enough to ride the bus across town, much less go looking for baked goods. "Not today." Maybe when he's become more comfortable with his prosthetic they could go out.

"That's all right, let's just get home and get you settled in. It's not much, my place, but it's affordable and pest free." For the last three days Huan has been saying some variety of that on regular intervals, giving him the impression that his boyfriend is a little embarrassed to not live somewhere nice. As far as Arthur is concerned, it doesn't matter. If it meant he got to sleep next to Huan and spend every day with him he'd live in a tent next to a landfill.

"I used to have a roommate, but he got married so now I'm trying to pay for it all on my own which is a bit hard, I've had to dip into my savings to make ends meet since I took time off to come see you every day. No more vacation time, but it was worth it. I think between the two of us it should be fine. I'll even cut down on the weed so we can save a bit of money there," he rambles on, gesturing and jerking Arthur's arm around.

"It's all right," Arthur interrupts. "I don't want you worrying about my bills." The army is paying for most of them, it's the arm that's going to cost him most and all the therapy that comes after. The VA might say they'll cover it but Arthur has little faith he'll be that lucky. He'll pay for it all somehow.

"But I want to help," Huan says, sticking out his bottom lip and giving Arthur an immediate urge to kiss him. So he does. A quick peck has his boyfriend smiling again, leaning against his side while the bus pulls up to the curb.

"You're helping plenty already," Arthur says when they've sat down.

Already getting tired, Arthur places his head on Huan's shoulder in favor of having his teeth rattled by the window. He's barely settled down before a hand is combing through his hair and a kiss is pressed to his forehead.

"Please let me take care of you, Arthur."

He has a feeling that this is a losing battle and he'd be better off cutting his losses for now, the bus isn't a good place to have an argument about this. Sighing, he closes his eyes, the rumble of the bus and hiss of hydraulics keeping him from simply drifting off.

Someone coming on at the next stop scoffs at them when they pass by and the implication of their opinion of him and Huan stings – until Huan makes a fart noise at them which is so wonderfully childish Arthur can't help but laugh, opening his eyes to see the offended look on the woman's face. Still, he tries to sit up, stopping short when Huan's hand in his hair keeps him where he is.

He feels a little put on the spot, but he knows Huan is in the right, they shouldn't have to hide who they are. No one else around them bats an eye, the woman moving on with a disgusted sneer. It doesn't keep shame from working into his mind and whispering doubts in his ear, all those things that Emmet has said to him over the years about being unnatural and going to hell for it. It'll take him a long time to recover from that.

HUAN CAN TELL ARTHUR IS SORTING THROUGH A LOT IN HIS MIND, AND the rest of the bus ride home is spent in silence. He can't blame him; Arthur has been through a lot in the last few weeks, not to mention the rest of his life. Huan can't even begin to imagine what it must be like having to live with it all.

What he can do is offer comfort when Arthur needs it, and space when he needs that.

When they get off at their stop he can practically feel Arthur's relief. Keeping his grip on the prosthetic arm, Huan starts leading him up the street towards his shabby little building where his landlady is sweeping the steps.

She grumbles at them for tracking in more dirt but smiles all the same, waving them along. She must be in a good mood today.

"It's not much but I like it here," Huan says for what feels like the hundredth time. To Arthur he must sound like a broken record, but he doesn't want him to be disappointed when their apartment doesn't turn out to be a modern piece of art. Everything in there is old and second hand, even his bong. Who can afford to buy new furniture these days?

"I swear it's all right, I used to live in a trailer with my brother, I ain't expecting a palace," Arthur mumbles in that charming drawl of his and Huan melts a little under the smooth whiskey sound of his boyfriend's voice.

Still scared that it's not enough he lets go of Arthur's hand to unlock the scuffed door and let them in. "Let me give you the grand tour." He makes a sweeping gesture at the modest apartment. "This is the kitchen slash living room, the bathroom is on your left next to the master bedroom, and on the right is the guest bedroom. I wasn't sure if you wanted to share my room or not so I made up the bed in the guest room too." *Please stay with me,* Huan silently prays. Words can not describe how badly he wants Arthur in his bed so they can finally sleep next to each other and with each other when that becomes an option again.

The few seconds where Arthur is silent, looking around the apartment from where they're still standing by the door, are excruciatingly long, "I want to share yours if that's all right?" he says, at long last.

Letting out the breath he'd been holding, Huan smiles, kneeling down to help Arthur get his boots off before carefully taking hold of Arthur's arm and walking him into their bedroom so they can unpack what little he has in his duffel bag. It barely fills half of one of the drawers he'd cleared out and Huan decides that as soon as Arthur feels up to it they have to buy him some more. Until then he could always get him some basics so he'll have clothes to wear at home.

"Are you hungry?" he asks to break the awkward tension that's crept in over them.

"Yup, I reckon so," Arthur replies, shifting on his feet and reaching up to lay his hand on the shoulder of his prosthetic. "Can you help me get this off first?"

Charmed that Arthur trusts him to help with something like that, Huan closes the gap between them to work open the buttons of his shirt, slowly exposing healing burns and bandages. It might not be conventional but to Huan he's beautiful, he's never known his soldier's body in any other way and he feels no regret over it. Scars make no difference, Arthur is still Arthur.

Once he has the shirt off he drops it to the side and presses a soft kiss by the edge of a bandage just because he can and he wants to. He taps lightly on the forearm of the prosthetic, "Let's get this off, then."

He'd been there every step of the way when they were fitting it and knows how it works, but he's still scared of hurting Arthur by doing it wrong. Carefully he opens the buckle, holding onto the arm so it'll stay in place until he has the strap entirely off and can ease it off with no problem. "There," he smiles, laying the arm down on the bed.

"Thank you, sweetheart," Arthur mumbles and smiles so softly, the corners of his full lips pulling up just so.

Knowing they're alone, Huan rises up on his tiptoes to kiss him without fear of being walked in on, pausing the clock to memorize the feeling of that smile against his own. Arthur melts into it, a big, warm hand coming up to rest on his lower back. He feels safe here with Arthur's comforting presence curled over him, giving him new confidence to say that they're going to be all right, they'll make it through this together.

BO STARSKY

Digging Holes and Ditches

"WHAT ARE YOU GOOD FOR?"

It's impersonal, just how Dov likes it, how it should be. Every alley encounter he's had has been like this, shoved up against the wall behind a Dumpster. It's the safest way for someone like him. His intentions with coming here from the Midwest had been to get away from anyone who knew him, so he could have this little freedom.

"Anything." Curt and to the point, rough and anonymous. Best not get attached.

"Let me fuck that ass." The one time a year he does this Dov preps himself with generous amounts of lube, tucks a condom into his pocket, and walks across town to one of the gay bars. He leaves his usual flannel at home in favor of a black t-shirt and leather jacket, something that doesn't look like him, anything to lessen the risk of being recognized by another cop. Then he lets himself get fucked, or fucks some pretty boy out behind the bar, before getting piss drunk to forget the whole thing.

It's what's best in the long run. Tomorrow's his birthday, he's turning thirty-seven and he's been doing it this way since he was twenty-one and moved away from home.

It used to be different, though: when he was younger and more reckless he'd do this nearly every weekend, then he went from being a uniform to a detective and he was no longer as anonymous. Once a month, every other, twice a year, once a year. It may be 1976 and a "new America," but he's still a queer and it's all he can risk at this stage.

His hook-up tugs violently at Dov's belt; he looks like an ordinary family man giving in to his vice, blue eyes and blond hair, bland, and a little too drunk and overconfident. He's just handed over the foil-wrapped condom when they hear someone. Dov's heart leaps into his throat, fight or flight making him too scared to hear what's said. In a flash his hook-up turns on him.

"Fucking faggot!" A fist catches him in the cheek, grazing off his nose. It's not much of a punch, angled awkwardly and too close to do much damage, but it surprises him enough that the man gets away, leaving Dov to whatever fate awaits him.

"Shit!" Someone is running up to him and he does the only thing he can think of, throwing his arms up to shield his head and praying to God that whoever it is doesn't have a gun.

But the footsteps pass, light slaps on the rain-wet concrete, following his trick until they suddenly stop a few feet away. He could run, he should. He could also pretend he's undercover, but that's a weak excuse, not to mention it would give away his identity as a cop.

"You okay?" Why does that voice sound so damn familiar? "Dov?" Hearing his own name pinpoints it.

Charles fucking Coleman. Who else would it be but the black supercop of Boulder, Colorado?

Dov's already been made so there's no point in hiding; this is it then, he survived fucking drug rings and gangs only to end up dead in an alley by the hands of someone he thought was a friend.

"Whatever you're going to do, just get it over with. Shoot me, beat me up, rat me out, just do it." Hands shaking, he taps a cigarette out thinking he'd like at least one last smoke before his life goes to shit.

There's no scenario in which this ends well for him.

"I'm not going to hurt you." Chuck sounds offended that he'd even imply such a thing.

"Why?" Dov looks up, he knows the weak streetlight makes his white skin look sickly. "I know what you saw."

All of this could have been avoided if he'd just tried harder to be normal instead of having this stupid indulgence. Almost as an afterthought he zips his jeans back up; no point in his corpse looking indecent when they find his body with a bullet or two lodged in him somewhere.

"I didn't see anything." Chuck smiles disarmingly, putting his hands up in a sign of peace, *deescalate*. Always the good cop. "Just some guy punching my friend in the face for no good reason." Chuck steps closer and Dov can't conceal the automatic flinch in the face of expected danger.

"What are you doing out here anyway?" The nicotine helps soothe his anxiety if only a little; he'd like to go back inside and proceed to the black-out drunk portion of the night, but as long as Chuck is standing there looking concerned he won't go anywhere.

In some ways it's making him a little uncomfortable, that concern, he doesn't understand why it's there. Chuck understands oppression, Dov knows that, but he isn't about to compare homophobia to centuries of racism and slavery, they're very different things and one is decidedly worse because it can't be hidden. As long as he keeps his mouth shut the worst crime Dov is guilty of is being Jewish, Chuck doesn't have the option to hide the color of his skin or the kink in his hair. Chuck's worst crime is just being alive in America.

"Had a date, didn't go well. Not for either of us, I suppose." You can say that again. For all of his shady hook-ups none of them have gone far enough to actually hurt him, most wouldn't dare once he stands up to his full height. He's lucky in that sense. Broad shoulders and the ability to look down on most men has been a benefit in many situations, just not this one it would seem.

"What do you want, Chuck?" If he isn't going to rat him out then he must have extortion on his mind, it's just too far-fetched that a straight man has nothing against Dov's proclivities. A fairytale concept. He's never lucky like that.

"I want to buy you a beer and offer you my leftover lasagna."
What?

"It's the least I can do for interrupting your, uh, date."

Okay, if that's how it is, fine, he'll suck a dick to keep his job and stay alive. Not exactly the kind of sex he was going for when he left home tonight, but he can live with that for the sake of staying straight in the eyes of his friends and co-workers.

However when they get to Chuck's place and all he does is slap a bag of frozen peas onto Dov's bruised face and shove a plate full of lasagna in the microwave, Dov is left more confused than ever. No one is this nice to a queer, not even Charles fucking Coleman. Something is going to happen; the anticipation is chewing on the lining of his gut and he's starting to worry it'll eat right through him if whatever *is* going to happen doesn't come to fruition soon.

The microwave beeps and a heap of salad goes next to the steaming pasta before it's deposited in front of him with a smile. At first Dov just stares suspiciously, flickering between the food and his friend, waiting for the other shoe to drop.

"The closest thing to a vegetable I've seen you eat is ketchup." Chuck must assume he's taken offence to the pile of green. Dov still doesn't believe this is real, but he relinquishes his peas in exchange for a fork and digs in. Might as well eat, maybe it'll stop the churning in his stomach.

The TV gets switched on in the ensuing silence, Johnny Carson conducting an interview in the background, until the plate is empty and Dov still can't find words to say. Should he just get on his knees or wait to be prompted? They continue on in excruciating silence for another twenty minutes before his anticipation gets the better of him. Despite popular opinion he never was a big fan of Carson and he's hardly enough to distract him away from this pit of quicksand he's slowly sinking into.

Dov clears his throat. "So...what do you want?" His voice cracks and he can't bring himself to raise his eyes from the table, studying the wood grain while he waits. He's ready for anything, so in essence Chuck can ask for whatever he wants and Dov can't say no, not this time.

"I want my friend to be okay." There he goes again with those impossible answers. "I don't care if you're gay and I'm sure as shit not going to take advantage of you."

Oh. There is no other shoe, unbelievable as it is. He's safe here, free to be himself for the first time in his life. A friend who truly knows him and still cares, and he doesn't even have to act like he's interested in women.

Dov's never once admitted to his own sexuality since his father beat him black and blue for kissing a boy when he was thirteen, threatening to send him to one of those conversion camps to *"Make you normal."* Not even to himself has he really admitted it, too scared that someone would read it in his face, notice how he doesn't leer at women or keep a copy of Playboy in his desk like everyone else, so he can stare at the centerfold with the rest of the guys or while eating his lunch. And now here he is, safe for the first time in two decades. It lightens a load he's gotten so used to carrying that he can feel how tired his soul is from hiding.

Chuck smiles softly, watching Dov sort through his thoughts over the mouth of a bottle of Coors.

"How are you so nice?" is all he can think to say in the end. "Anyone else would have skinned me alive by now."

Despite the fact that he's possibly gotten away scot-free from something that could have been the end of him, he's still tempted to offer himself up. He came out tonight with a goal and now it's too late to go elsewhere if he wants to be functional in the morning; Chuck is his only viable option.

There must be a line somewhere that he has yet to cross, there always is. But where's that line right now?

"I'll still suck your dick if you want." He figures he can blame the beer he's absolutely not had enough of if shit goes sideways and Chuck decides to put him in his place.

This has the potential to go very horribly wrong; propositioning a straight man is a dangerous game. Even if Chuck says yes Dov doesn't expect anything in return, if you close your eyes a mouth is like any other, but it ruins the illusion if a second dick gets involved. He learned that the hard way. He stopped messing around with straight men after that.

"I consider myself a traditional man, I like to take things slow."

Well, it's the nicest rejection he's been served, he's okay with that.

"How about we start with this?" Chuck takes him by surprise yet again, this time by stepping up to the dining table, and bending down to lay one on him.

Dov's second kiss of the night is long and slow, a stark difference from the violent biting and rushed collision of teeth he's used to, Chuck even lets him lead. It all makes him wonder for a second if he's drunker than he thought, but two beers is nowhere near enough to make him dream like this.

For once in his life he decides not to look a gift horse in the mouth and just take whatever Chuck is willing to give him. They do end up in the bedroom, after all, and that's where Dov starts getting nervous again. He's never had sex in a bed before, the closest he's ever got being the backseat of a car, where it's dark and anonymous. This room is so obviously Chuck's, it has personality in its little knick knacks and features, cozy and lived in.

He still doesn't know what to expect, what Chuck wants from him. Making the decision for him would be best, he'll drop his jeans and bend over, that way Chuck won't have to look at him beyond his ass and maybe he'll get through this without losing a friend. He won't have to look at Chuck either, he can hide his face in his arms and act like he hasn't been wanting Chuck to fuck him since they first met, like he hasn't brought himself off to the idea on the regular.

How could he not?

Chuck had been striking from day one, sauntering into that meeting like he wasn't the rookie they needed for a racially sensitive matter. They wouldn't be able to pull it off without him and he'd known that. To Dov none of that had mattered because a beautiful man had just walked into the room, his dark skin glowing enticingly under the fluorescents that always seem to wash out Dov's own. There was no way on God's green earth that Dov could have kept his mind from wandering to that charming smile or those skilled hands.

Now here he is, kissing that mouth while those hands feel him up, and he has no idea what to do about it.

The amount of space available to him is a welcome change even if he knows he won't use it, knows he'll keep his arms and legs to himself, take up the least amount of room he can. Best not to leave a mark, make it easier for Chuck to forget this ever happened.

He's about to untangle himself from another kiss and get into position when Chuck makes swift work of Dov's jacket and starts pulling his shirt up. It's unexpected, most men don't even bother with undressing him more than to expose the right parts and, like the bed, he's never had sex fully naked, there's never been time. This is so far away from what he's used to, and he's starting to feel like Chuck is the only thing keeping him from falling off the precipice while at the same time pushing him closer to the edge. This could either end in disaster or turn out to be the best sex he's ever had.

With his chest bare he feels horribly exposed, fighting the urge to cover up. It's one thing to be seen undressed in the locker room, but standing here with his dick hard in his friend's bedroom is an entirely different scene. And he is hard, rock solid and straining, he would be embarrassed about it if Chuck wasn't sporting too, which is another unexpected factor. He wasn't expecting Chuck to get hard before Dov got face down, ass up, so he could do his thing and cover up again, acting like nothing has happened.

He's had a few guys wanting it like that, acting like it isn't real if he never sees their dick, wanting him to stay still like a toy. In the heat of the moment he's grateful Chuck isn't like that, he's not sure he could handle it if he was, it's going to be difficult enough to move on from this as is.

Chuck guides him down onto the bed before stepping back to relieve himself of his clothes. Dov turns his back, yanking his stupid bellbottoms down and taking position. The sheets smell like Chuck, like coconut and spices, and he thinks for a moment that maybe he won't be able to go through with this.

"Is doing it this way what you want or what you think I want?"

He hadn't realized how quiet it had got before Chuck said that, a warm hand smoothing down Dov's tense back.

"You tell me." Speaking is a lot harder than he expected it to be, his voice coming out rough like sandpaper.

A kiss lands on his neck just below the cut of his hair, Chuck's skin warm against his back, chest hair scratching at his skin just right. "I think," another kiss, "it's time," another, "someone took care of you for once." A push at his hip is all it takes for Dov to tumble sideways, leaving him on display for Chuck to see.

His jeans are gone before he has time to process what's happening; suddenly he's naked and Chuck is settling between his legs, pressing him down into the bed. This is something new as well, he's always done it with his back turned for the sake of convenience. He's never had to look someone in the face while feeling their cock pressed against his own.

Despite the change in position he still expects this to be a quick affair, but Chuck keeps surprising him by leaning down to mouth at his neck, firm hands touching him in places he's never been touched. There is no hard grip on his hips, no nails biting into his skin, it's soft in a way he's convinced himself he could never have.

By the time he catches his moan it's too late, it's already out there and he can't take it back, Chuck hums back from where he's sucking on Dov's collarbone. "Let me hear you, baby," he reassures, speaking to the flushed skin of Dov's chest; he rolls his hips once, coaxing out another soft groan. "Yeah, that's it, baby."

When a warm mouth closes over his nipple Dov's cock twitches where it's pressed between their bellies. On his own he's always liked playing with his nipples, but having someone else do it is a gift he should have asked for sooner, even the rough scratch of facial hair is shooting sparks up his spine. It's almost too much, the need for more tingling in his stomach.

"Please," he finally begs, he's barely hanging on, teetering on the edge of letting go, of letting himself enjoy this fully.

Chuck listens, reaching between them to rub at Dov's hole, pushing the tip of a finger in to pull at the rim.

"Please."

Just when Dov thinks he can't take it any more Chuck reaches into his bedside table coming out with a tube of KY. He shudders in anticipation, too far gone to care how he looks or sounds. This is what he needs.

While Chuck slicks himself up Dov makes a motion to turn

over again. Chuck stops him before he can get more than a third of the way there, pushing him back onto the bed with a kiss that takes his breath away. It's there, while Dov is swimming in dazed arousal, that Chuck pushes into him.

Dov's entire body sings with the sensation, arching up in search of more contact that he's given freely. There's not a single complaint while he clings to Chuck, trying so hard to hold on to that damned edge while Chuck rocks into him at a steady rhythm, sparks zipping up Dov's spine with each thrust.

He's been ruined, Chuck has made sure of that, the chance he'll ever have something like this again is slim to none. "Just let go," a voice whispers to him and it takes him a while to realize that it's Chuck. "I've got you, baby, it's okay."

Dov lets go.

He falls.

It feels like it'll never stop, his body convulsing, vision turning white. How could he have missed out on this for so long?

Chuck's hips stutter and he goes to pull back. "No," Dov mumbles through the haze, closing his legs tight around Chuck's waist, pushing him deeper until there's just enough space for Chuck to rut against him. He wants something to remember this by, something he's never let anyone else do.

Sated, spent, and covered in a layer of sweat, Dov holds on just long enough for Chuck to finish before allowing himself to slump. Body still twitching with aftershocks, he barely even notices Chuck sliding down next to him, pulling the covers up over them.

The next thing he knows he's waking up to the smell of coffee and cooking bacon, body pleasantly aching. Chuck singing along to Sam & Dave drifts in on the pale Sunday morning sun reasserting that last night really did happen, that Chuck made him come so hard he practically passed out.

Well, shit.

That had been everything and more than his fantasies could ever have provided him with, gentle in ways he's never known and so damn intense he still can't think straight. Because of course Charles fucking Coleman would be the guy to blow Dov's mind. Would be the first to pick him apart like that and prove that it doesn't have to be the way he's laid it out for himself. And now he has no fucking clue what to do about it.

This isn't something he ever made a contingency plan for because why would he ever have sex with a coworker or a friend, with someone he knows? Not to mention he probably screamed loud enough to wake the whole building, he can't fucking remember, last night still draped in a haze of bliss. He should get dressed and leave before he gets thrown out, avoid that awkward conversation he really doesn't want to have. It'll be better for them both if they can just move on and act like this never happened.

He's pretty sure he came here wearing clothes, but when he gets up to look there are none, not that belong to him, anyway. Now what?

He can't run out of here stark naked with dried come on his chest, a hickey on his collarbone, and hair resembling a crow's nest without raising a few eyebrows. He could nab the sheets, but he doubts Chuck would let him walk out of here with them.

Speak of the devil.

"I figured you'd try to run so I took the liberty of washing your clothes." Chuck smiles at him from the doorway and Dov automatically goes to cover himself with his hands.

"I won't tell anyone about this." Who would he tell anyway?

"That's not what I'm worried about." The fact that Chuck isn't wearing a shirt makes him feel slightly better about his own nudity. "I'm worried that you're going to run off and dig yourself into a hole about this."

Oh.

"I've already started." Dov's whole life is full of holes like that, what's one more?

"Then let me stop you." Dov accepts the kiss as it comes, leaning down into it, basking in Chuck's hidden talent of making him forget how to worry for a little while. That's all he needs.

Except something is different now, brand new and standing on shaky legs like a newborn foal that's ready to grow strong and endure years of hard work.

Dov couldn't have predicted this would happen, less than a year since Chuck sauntered into his life wearing corduroy bellbottoms and a satin shirt unbuttoned just enough to hint at the dark fur covering his chest. He figures he could call it the best birthday present he's ever gotten, though that won't be quite right because over the years Chuck keeps blowing his mind for every birthday after, even on the days in between.

They didn't know it at the time, but that morning they made a promise to try, a promise they keep for decades to come. All because of a single coincidence that took place in the summer of '76.

It's funny how the best things in life happen when you least expect them.

How to Grab His Attention:
A Guide to Getting Your Man

EZRA HAS NEVER MADE ANY SECRET OF THE FACT THAT HE'S BI.

He likes sex too much to just limit himself to one gender, and the fact of it is he can get twice as much ass as a straight guy could. And, in that same vein, not one of his multitude of siblings would ever hesitate to call him a slut; which he is, unashamedly.

One thing Ezra isn't is a regular purveyor of books, but here he is, lurking around the shelves of the new bookshop that opened last week in the town centre. In the year of our Lord, two-thousand-and-eighteen, Ezra can remember having read three entire books from cover to cover since he was a teen, all of them mandatory school reading. Now he's well into his twenty-fifth year of life and trying to figure out how he's going to flirt with the clerk, who looks like a snack in his sharp uniform. Before today he hadn't even known they had uniforms in bookshops. Regardless of whether they do or don't, this one does, and the guy at the register looks like it was designed with him in mind.

The entire shop is posh and upmarket, the kind of place his mom would call charming and fashionable, then possibly fresh when she'd discover the adult section in the back. So far it's Ezra's favorite section, and he's picked up a Kama Sutra in a not-so-subtle effort to let the guy know he wants to get his nose between those cheeks and blow raspberries on his probably-pornstar-pink asshole.

Him lurking around the shelves copping looks at the slim brunette probably isn't helping his chances, but he's hoping for a clue to something he might like. But the guy doesn't *do* anything, he just works. Imagine being at work and actually working, who does that?

The book about boning in acrobatic ways doesn't work, the hottie whose name tag says Vincent rings it up without batting an eye at Ezra's smirk and wink combo, putting it in a bag and wishing him a good day. He'll just have to try harder then.

Sitting on his computer Googling suggestive book titles isn't something Ezra thought he'd ever do, though it's not something that would be out of character for him if he thinks about it. It's an unconventional way of flirting and he hopes Vincent will appreciate it because he's making more of an effort than just walking up and saying it right to his face. Not that there's anything wrong with that. Ezra has had plenty of success by being straightforward. It's just that for some reason this feels a little different. Maybe it's because Vincent is older than the men he usually goes for, a tasteful hint of grey at his temples, and a to-die-for French accent.

It turns out that there are plenty of books he could order that might convey the message, now he just needs to decide if he should tell Vincent all the things he wants him to do to him or be more sweet and romantic. It's hard to tell what the guy might enjoy. To be or not to be horny, that is the question.

He'll try romantic first; once he starts being horny there's usually no way back.

So next week he goes to the bookshop again, wondering if there are people who go to bookshops every week in real life or if he's being weird. This time he's browsing the romance section, looking at the titles and trying to find something that will make sense.

Today there are two employees in the store, both wearing that clean cut trouser and waistcoat combo; usually he'd be dreaming of a threesome right about now, him sandwiched between Vincent and the top-heavy blonde that's sorting through a box of books. But as pretty as she is, Ezra's eye stays drawn to Vincent and how he looks like he was sewn into that uniform.

And still not being a regular purveyor of bookshops he doesn't really understand *why* there's a uniform. A dress code, sure, but a mandatory, fancy-schmancy uniform? Then again this is a suburban area full of white people and hipsters, so maybe it's not that strange.

It's been a while since Ezra has lived here, but in the aftermath of getting fired for accidentally hitting on his boss he's had to take up residence in his widowed mother's basement, aka: his childhood bedroom. That had been one of the few perks of being the baby. With all his older siblings gone off to college or moved out, teenaged him was allowed to claim the basement that used to be a rec center for them all. A few Playboy centerfolds and an iconic poster of Jeff Goldblum lounging sexily in an open shirt later and the place felt like his own.

Those posters are still there and get him off just as good as they did a decade ago.

But back to the current mission of getting the handsome man into his bed.

Ezra is starting to feel a little awkward because he's been pretending to browse for a little too long to be normal. Knowing he can't stay in here any longer, he picks a book for the title alone: *Hot Stuff*. Taking it up to the register he makes sure to put it down so Vincent can easily read the title.

He rings it up without so much as a glance. "That'll be fourteen ninety-nine," he requests, and defeated by professionalism yet again, Ezra hands him a twenty and tells him to keep the change.

He's almost out the door, stuffing a new cigarette between his lips, before he stops short, holding up a finger and turning around. "Just one more thing." He trots back up to the counter trying to remember the title of that book.

"Yes, Detective Columbo, how may I help you?" Columbo? Snatching the cigarette from his lips Ezra jams it in his pocket, clearing his throat awkwardly.

"I wanted to order a book."

They stare at each other in silence for a moment.

"And what would that book be called?" Vincent prompts.

"Uhhh–" Ezra dawdles, scraping the surface of his apparently useless brain for the title of a book, any book so he'll have an excuse to come back. "How to Get Him to Notice You? Or something like that?" Why is making an effort so hard? He's never this awkward at flirting.

Vincent hums, typing inhumanly fast on the computer before looking back up. "I can get you one called *How to Grab His Attention: A Guide to Getting Your Man?*" Ezra very badly wants to cringe at the title and how it almost sounds decent in Vincent's accent, who would have thought he'd ever be buying self-help books? If his mother ever finds out about this her constant digging into his personal affairs is likely going to increase tenfold. It's bad enough that she snoops through his room on the regular. As a parent she had no boundaries and that apparently extends into his adult life when he's fully capable of caring for himself. Says the man living in his mother's basement.

Trying not to make a face, Ezra nods, "That's the one."

"We can have it for you next week?"

"Sure." His voice comes out a little strained and he's definitely blushing with the humiliation of having to do this, if only it wasn't his own fucking fault he's in this position in the first place. Throwing a hastily mumbled thanks over his shoulder, Ezra makes his escape, pulling up his collar against the wind and rooting around his pocket for his cigarette that's now bent.

Sighing, he lights it anyway, no point in wasting it.

Around him everyone gets on with their business, jogging between stores and their cars. It's a shame the weather is as poor as it is because he can't drive his car with the top down, what's the point of a convertible sports car if you can't drive it top down? He'd like to think he didn't waste his hard-earned money on a frivolous status symbol he can't use to its full potential. Owning a Porsche screams successful, the one thing he kind of isn't.

Sure, he went to college, got his degree and a great job; but what good does that do when he's shit at finances and keeping said job. Successful people don't live in their mother's basements. His siblings are all better off than he is because, on top of being the baby by quite a few years, he's the black sheep.

A hot temper and a brain wired to be constantly horny does not a success make.

Were she alive his bubbe would be ashamed.

Vincent looks successful, now that he thinks about it, with the uniform, his neatly slicked hair, and upper-class, French accent. He's exactly the kind of put-together man Ezra has always had a desire to bring down to his level. Except he doesn't want to do that to Vincent.

Vincent doesn't act like he's above him, he treats him the same as every other customer with that impeccable smile that has him so charmed. What Ezra wants to do to him is take him out for dinner and show him a good time, but he wants to do it right and maybe that's why he hasn't gone for any of his usual methods. His pursuit of the bookshop silver fox might actually teach him some new tricks past his natural charm that he rarely uses for good.

Not going to the bookshop for an entire week is harder than it has any right to be and Ezra is starting to fear that he's becoming a nerd. He makes it, distracting himself with trying to find a new job, because his eldest brother refuses to let him into the family business – as if he's the reigning monarch of small town sporting goods. It's not like Ezra wants to work there anyway, he made it through college, barely, he has a degree and opportunities. He likes to think, anyway.

Finding work is harder than it has any right to be, Ezra filling the time between applications with jerking off way too much, and making a valiant effort at spanking himself while imagining it to be Vincent. Oh, the things he'd let that man do to him. Spanking is just the start of a very long list of debauchery that would make a whore blush and require an entire vat of lube if his usage this week is anything to go by.

His mom is offering plenty of motivation with her nosiness though. How come it's so hard for her to *not* dig around in his stuff? Being a shrink is no excuse and, personally, he thinks she ought to leave that at the office – especially since she's retired. If he wanted to be psychoanalyzed at every turn he'd pay for it. Now that he thinks about it, maybe he should.

"Where are you going?"

Ezra pauses midway through pulling on his jacket, looking back at the blonde head of hair poking out of the kitchen doorway.

"Out." He's a grown man, for Christ's sake, can't he leave the house without an interrogation?

"If it's to get more lube I already got you some, better than the one you had, too. You should look after your toys." That's not something he ever wanted to hear his sixty-two year old mother say. Clearly he needs about twenty padlocks on his toy box to keep her out.

"No, but if you have to know I'm going to pick up a book I ordered." It's hardly a criminal offence, he's just a man trying to woo another man with awful books that have suggestive titles.

"Mr. Bell is straight, you know? He used to be married." *What?* Ezra hates how that little piece of information makes him feel.

"How do you know that?" He shrugs his jacket the rest of the way on, reaching up to sort out the collar.

"I asked." Leaving her position by the kitchen door she comes over to fix his collar for him, Ezra obediently bending down so she can reach. "He said they parted as friends."

Ezra scoffs; no one is friends with their ex, especially not their ex-wife. "I've been with girls, does that mean I'm straight too?" He refuses to believe a man as well-groomed as Vincent is strictly a pescatarian. Not to mention his colorful waistcoat buttons that just so happen to make a rainbow.

"I just don't want you to get hurt, honey, that's all." Pleased with her work on his collar she pats him on the cheek, giving him a little push towards the door.

"Thanks, Mom." He's no stranger to rejection. Hell, he was rejected *and* fired in one fell swoop and he still doesn't carry any hard feelings over it. It sucks for sure, but it was his own fault to begin with so he really has no right to blame it on his boss.

"I know how you let your feelings get the better of you when you see someone you like," she continues, while Ezra reaches for the door. "Please think with your head for once." Yeah, he really needs to get out of here before she launches into some monologue about attachments, feelings, and misinterpreting physical attraction as something more. She means well, but he's heard it enough times already.

"See you later, Mom," he insists with a smile, escaping out the door and down to his car so he can go see if Vincent has caught on by now to what he's trying to do.

Walking in he's immediately met with a problem, a rather unexpected one. The door to the back room is open and he can hear Vincent firmly lecturing someone in that crisp accent of his and it's doing things to Ezra that are entirely inappropriate for the public. Suddenly hating his kink for authority he absconds into the shelves to hide from the other customers, snatching up the first book he can find to strategically carry it in front of his opportunistic erection.

"God, you're such a slut," he hisses at himself while his mind conjures up vivid fantasies about what could happen if Vincent was yelling at him. If he's completely honest with himself Ezra would let the man crush his kneecaps and punch him in the throat, though he'd much rather have Vincent dominate him and make him feel like a little bitch. It would be a lot more fun than broken bones. Such a shame it might never happen if his mother's assumption is correct, despite the clues suggesting otherwise.

As if cowed by this realization the throbbing in his crotch recedes, his erection giving up in the face of the near unclimbable cliff that is heterosexuality. Still, he has to try.

Hearing footsteps, he quickly rakes a hand through his hair and smoothes down his goatee, ignoring that he'd already looked in the rearview mirror of his car before coming inside and knows he looks good. Not that that's ever made a difference the other times he's been in here.

Replacing the book he'd used to hide behind, he strolls up to the register with as much confidence as he can muster, only to fall short when it's the tall blond woman that greets him. *Damn it.* Now there are two people in the word that know he's ordered a hideously embarrassing book and he doesn't even get to use it for its intended purpose.

What a load of crap.

"Here to pick up your book, sir?" she asks all politely, ignoring

Ezra's red face with that dead-eyed look that comes as a result of working in retail. He's all too familiar with it, having seen it on his brother for years. Nothing scares him more than retail and service workers, because he knows for a fact they will fight you and show no remorse. He got that from his brother, too. Mom still hasn't forgiven them for breaking several of her collectible china plates that one time.

Ezra sighs, "Yeah." He puts a crumpled twenty on the counter, trying to look anywhere but at her face as she exchanges the bill for a self-help book with a cheery cover of a confident-looking woman and a handsome man. He can't wait to shove that under his bed and never look at it again.

By the fifteenth time he's been there, Ezra is starting to get a little frustrated and has amassed a small stack of books with suggestive titles he's never going to read. Except for maybe *How to Grab His Attention,* he could use the advice right about now. He might just have to admit defeat at the hands of his dreaded enemy: heterosexuality.

One last time, he'll try one last time.

The worst thing about this whole charade is that during his extended effort to woo Vincent, Ezra has gone from thinking he's hot to having a massive crush the likes of which he hasn't experienced since high school. A crush is almost always bad news for it'll make it that much more painful when he's inevitably rejected, the odds of success are too small to be worth it. Yet he has to try *one more time.*

"Good afternoon, Ezra," Vincent greets him without even looking up from where he's putting new books on the shelf, giving Ezra an amazing view of his ass in those pinstripe slacks. "Placing an order or just browsing?" he asks, as if he doesn't know Ezra never leaves empty handed.

"Just browsing." Giving Vincent's ass one last look Ezra heads for the adult section. He could swear Vincent does that on purpose, it's as if he knows he's being watched when he crouches down like that.

Halfheartedly browsing the well-stocked section Ezra tries to find something that no one would be able to ignore or not catch the meaning of, the raunchier the better. If this is going to be the last attempt he's going out with a bang.

The book he chooses has two dark haired men on the cover, locked in a passionate embrace under the cheesy title of *Love Me all Night*. It's not dirty, but it's the best he's found so far, and if that's not a clear message, Ezra doesn't know what is. Vincent just *has* to go for this one, he has to.

Gripping the book tightly enough that the paper cover buckles a little, Ezra takes it up to the register where Vincent is already waiting, customer service smile firmly in place. Like every other fucking time he doesn't so much as blink, scanning the book and putting it in a little paper bag. "Will that be all?"

For a hot second Ezra is about to lay it all out as it is, but no one is so obtuse they won't have caught on to what he's doing. Vincent has been ignoring every move he's made and it's time for Ezra to admit defeat, throw in the towel, cry uncle, etc. He's done. Closing his mouth Ezra's teeth click together and he purses his lips before shaking his head.

Then Vincent sighs, his polite smile turning into something softer that makes Ezra's heart skip a beat. "You could have just asked."

What?

"What?"

"Did you know your mother told me to let you down easy?"

Ezra squints suspiciously, suddenly very confused about this whole thing. "She did?"

"I wasn't going to." He shakes his head, a few strands of dark auburn hair coming loose and looking ridiculously tantalizing where they settle over his brow. "I figured you'd eventually just ask instead of continuing your adorably stupid game."

"You knew the whole time?" There's not much that can make Ezra blush, but knowing that Vincent has been letting him make a fool of himself for weeks is plenty humiliating. He feels about five seconds away from curling up on the floor and crying a single manly tear.

"Perhaps not until your mother gave it away, she told me you're stubborn and have a, uh, 'generous appetite,' but also you're sensitive and full of emotion," Vincent relays with a shit eating grin that lets Ezra know he's plenty capable of holding his own – and that his mother likes to overshare with fucking everyone. "Then she threatened me that if I was going to keep breaking your heart, she'd send your brothers to beat me up."

"Oy vey," Ezra sinks into a crouch and covers his burning face with his hands, "I can't believe my mom pretty much called me a slut." Not that she's wrong.

There's a slight creak of wood and a whisper of cloth as Vincent leans over the counter. "Are you all right down there?"

"Yeah," Ezra breathes out in a mighty gust, standing back up and uncovering his face, "I'm fine." Okay, this isn't the worst case scenario. He'd hoped it would be a lot smoother and more charming than this, but his mom's talent for meddling got in the way. He can recover from this.

"Well, then, are you going to stop buying books you won't read and just ask?"

"Are you going to say yes if I do?"

Vincent raises a perfectly-plucked brow which speaks for him.

"Can I buy you a drink?" Hope colors his voice, though he fears the worst.

"No. You and I both know that's not what either of us want. What you can do is come with me upstairs." Vincent smirks, casually waving the hot blonde over to take his place as if he didn't just invite Ezra to almost-certainly fuck, like a scene out of a porno.

How does something like this even happen in real life?

Following Vincent through to the back of the store and up a flight of stairs, Ezra is starting to wonder what exactly he's agreed to. He's sure it'll be good, less so that it's smart. He's been chasing after Vincent for so long now and losing hope along the way, so now that they're about to do this he's lost all sight of anything resembling a plan.

Apparently he needn't have worried. The moment the door to the upstairs apartment is open Ezra is being yanked inside by the collar of his jacket and pushed up against the wall in a searing kiss. He definitely hadn't been expecting that.

He'd had a plan to take Vincent out for a few drinks, lay the charm down thick, then they'd go back to his place and fuck like rabbits. In Vincent's version they seem to have skipped a few steps, mainly the part Ezra is actually good at. For as much sex as he has, he's never claimed to be a master at it, all he does is ask questions and listen to what his partners enjoy. Listening is a lot harder when a banging hottie with years of experience on him is pulling on his bottom lip with his pearly white teeth.

This is most definitely the best case scenario.

Not wanting to be run over entirely, Ezra hooks his hands under Vincent's pert ass and lifts, turning them around to press him up against the wall. Going by the surprised gasp and the way Vincent wraps around him, it was a good move.

"Wipe that smirk off your face, we only have thirty minutes to do this." The sharp tone of Vincent's voice is juxtaposed by the soft way he cups Ezra's face, pulling him back in for another kiss that steals his breath away. Having Vincent use that tone on him is hotter than anything he's imagined so far.

Not having had the chance to look around the room he doesn't dare try to move them somewhere else; with his luck he'd trip and they'd end this encounter at the ER. So he keeps them right where they are, breaking away to leave a trail of kisses along Vincent's jaw and down his neck to the starched collar of his shirt. If they had more time he'd peel that fucking uniform off with his teeth.

In the moment he has to settle for pulling the tie off and popping a few buttons so he can mark the pale skin hiding under his collar. He moans so beautifully when Ezra bites down, leaving behind a bloom of red. He wants to hear more.

Changing his grip he shuffles Vincent an inch lower, rolling his hips up and grinding his hardening cock against Vincent's answering erection – one he'd love to choke on.

"Clock's ticking, *mon chéri.*"

Ezra rolls his eyes at the reminder, grumbling, "Shut up," while trying not to let it show too much that he'll do anything Vincent asks of him.

If Vincent wants him to hurry up, he'll hurry.

Letting him back down Ezra goes for his belt, yanking it out of the loops and throwing it somewhere behind him. Next is the fly that has him cursing his hands for not being nimble enough to just grip the damn tab to pull the zipper down. It feels like he's wasted an eternity grappling with it before he finally gets hold and yanks it down.

Vincent is hard, the outline of his cock thick beneath the most pretentious underpants he's ever seen a man wear. "Is that silk?"

"Shut up."

Grinning like an idiot Ezra slips his hand below the elastic, finding Vincent to be waxed smooth and softer than the fucking silk boxers. Every few strokes he gets a new sound, a groan, a sigh, a moan, each and every one of them good motivation, and when he's just about to ask for a hand, Vincent beats him to the punch. What he gets isn't ideal, but he's not about to complain when they don't have time; instead he dives back in for a sloppy kiss and ruts against the thigh between his own. No, he's going to enjoy this as much as he can then walk away with a new contact in his phone.

This is the kind of sex you have in the bathroom of a bar at two am, Ezra realizes, as he frantically jerks Vincent off. Though he has to admit this is better due to no pounding music and neither of them being drunk. Bringing him out of his sudden woolgathering is the hand rubbing at him through his jeans and finally giving him some relief.

Arm getting tired from the brisk pace, Ezra gives himself a short break by focusing on the head alone, spreading the bead of slick there and rubbing his thumb against the glans.

"Do you have any idea how hot you look? Walking around in your fancy uniform looking like Mr. Darcy? I don't know if I want to fuck you or if I want you to spank me with a ruler." He's way past the point of caring how horny he sounds, why should it matter anyway when he has a dick in his hand?

"You're enough of a brat that I might," Vincent murmurs and Ezra revels in the breathless quality of his voice, a sure sign that he's getting close.

The hand on him tightens, making Ezra wish he could stop long enough to get his jeans off, but when he tries, Vincent gives him a look that says he better not. So he doesn't. It's become pretty clear that he's not getting off unless Vincent does.

In any other situation he'd complain, but he can't deny how worked up he is from being bossed around by an older man in a suit.

Figuring Vincent would appreciate the lack of a mess, Ezra sinks down on his knees and opens his mouth, intending to catch every drop. A hand fists in his hair, pulling him close enough for the head to rest on his tongue just before Vincent comes with a groan, throbbing in Ezra's hand. Try as he might some of it escapes him, streaking across his cheek, which he doesn't mind. It's such a tantalizing contrast between Vincent's clean-cut persona and the messiness of rushed sex, the splash of come warm against his skin.

Swallowing the rest, Ezra uses his tongue to clean Vincent's cock, swiping up the drop that clings to his slit. "You're quite something, aren't you?" Vincent drawls, running his thumb over Ezra's bottom lip. "Go ahead, touch yourself for me."

Though it's a little awkward to be put on the spot, Ezra is too turned on to care, finally yanking open his jeans and getting his cock out. Above him Vincent is tucking himself away, further tipping the scales of power.

Taking himself in hand Ezra makes sure to maintain eye contact as he strokes himself, perfectly aware of how debauched he looks. A soft and manicured hand comes down to cup his chin, keeping him in place to watch Vincent smile with satisfaction. "Be a good boy and come for Daddy."

And that's another new addition to his ever-expanding list of kinks, Ezra thinks, right before he comes. Eyes fluttering shut he gives himself over to the rush of ecstasy.

"Fuck," he breathes, listening to the patter of cum dripping on the hardwood floor.

"You came on the floor?" Vincent's incredulous tone cuts through the bliss like a knife and Ezra can't help laughing while tucking away his cock.

"You came on my face," he shoots back.

"I suppose that's fair – just clean it up."

"Yes, *Daddy*," Ezra winks, feeling like he's won the Powerball when Vincent blushes and gives him a *look*.

"Your mother really wasn't exaggerating, you are a slut." The soft smile Vincent gives him more than makes up for the harsh words, then to make it even better he pulls a handkerchief out of his pocket and wipes away the stray line of cum from Ezra's cheek.

And Ezra still can't believe that in a roundabout way his mom got him laid; he should buy her flowers or some shit.

"Now come on, off the floor." Taking his hands Vincent pulls him upright. "Get cleaned up, then it's time for you to go home, I won't have you taking me anywhere looking like that, much less smelling like cum. I'll see you downstairs."

A little slow to catch up on what's happening, Ezra openly stares at Vincent's ass while he bends to retrieve his tie and belt from the floor, giving in to temptation and reaching out for a feel. He can only grin at the look he gets back.

"I'll see you at seven." And with that Vincent takes his leave, leaving Ezra in his apartment all alone. If he's honest, Ezra wouldn't extend that level of trust to himself. Not that he'd ever steal anything, but Vincent doesn't know that.

Looking around the apartment a smile creeps onto his face; he has a date. Somehow his flirting approach worked. Isn't that something? And for once in his life he doesn't go snooping on his quest to find a tissue to clean the floor with, he only does what he's been told to do, he has a feeling it'll pay off later.

Floor and face clean, he lets himself out, pulling a cigarette out of the pack he carries in his pocket, and slipping down the stairs back into the shop where Vincent flags him down at the register. "I have something for you." A book thumps into his chest, and a hand snatches the unlit cigarette from his mouth, Vincent smiling politely all while ushering him towards the door.

Contrary to popular belief, Ezra can take a hint, letting himself back out onto the street where he pulls out a new cigarette; he'll be damned if he's going to quit because of a hook-up. However, before he can light it he looks back through the window to find Vincent leveling him with a disapproving stare. For a moment Ezra just stands there, lighter flickering out in the soft breeze. "Fuck!" Plucking the cigarette from his mouth he stuffs it back into his near empty pack of twenty. He can wait until he gets home.

It isn't until he's halfway to his car that he actually looks at the book Vincent gave him. The two-word title has him coming to a stop in the middle of the pavement, a smile starting as an uptick in the corner of his mouth turning into a full blown toothy grin. Emblazoned across a period-looking landscape in soft cursive is *Absolutely Smitten'*.

Then he opens it and finds an anti-smoking pamphlet.

"Motherfucker."

Copper Top

1

Though it has its own breed of strange, Ireland has nothing on London.

Eli's motivation for relocating to this urban landscape, where his biggest expense has become loose leaf tea, was to get away from the secluded small town station he served before, find a stable position with Scotland Yard, with a decent flat, in a safe borough – far from the modest corner of Ireland where he fit in about as well as you'd expect a gay man to do.

London has its upsides and downsides, crime is much more widespread and violent here, every illegal act you can imagine passing through a policeman's hands. Some end in tragedy, and those are the ones most difficult to leave behind. Eli considers himself lucky he's not in homicide.

The upside is all the unique characters he encounters on a regular basis. Stationed in Soho, there's no end to the things he would never have thought possible anywhere else. It's everything from the rich and famous seeking a little illicit fun to truly absurd street performers – a hodge podge of colorful people from all walks of life.

Before he moved here drag queens were something he'd only seen on TV and people he mostly perceived as pretty little twinks with a lisp, or aging chain smokers with clown makeup.

Nowhere in his expectations did he factor in a drag queen like Gloria Hole.

Gloria is an American queen so jacked she looks like she bench presses the whole swim team before breakfast. He's never seen Gloria out of drag because every time he's had the pleasure of her company she's been on the wrong side of the divider in his patrol car, usually blind drunk, angry, or an unholy combination of the two. Why the clubs keep hiring her he'll never know, but as long as they do he can expect to see her pale bulk at least once a week.

Always dressed to the nines in everything from elaborate gowns and costumes to as little as lingerie, Gloria never fails to impress with her looks. She is a sight to behold. He's not sure he even wants to see her out of drag at this point; it might shatter that lovely illusion of sharp cheekbones and pouty lips. Not to mention he would have to actually own up to just how attractive he finds her – what's under all that make-up has got to be just as stunning.

Tonight's outfit can only be described as a tube of latex with an ass window; Eli can't quite decide if it's intentional or if the outfit simply couldn't contain Gloria's smooth, pearly white behind. Right now the queen is dangerously close to throttling a guy who looks like a cast member of The Only Way is Essex. Much to the man's credit he hasn't shit himself yet, still edging for a fight despite the six-foot-three drag queen in thigh-high stiletto boots and acrylic nails that could pluck the eyes out of his skull.

"Guuurl, you gon catch these hands if you're not careful!" Gloria looms, widening her stance and executing an impressive hair flip that has the growing crowd cheering. Why is it always him who has to deal with this? Why can't Gloria pick fights when he isn't on duty? Then again, he'd like to see PC Ali try to handle her, she would bully him to tears in ten seconds flat.

Eli clears his throat. Best cool this down before someone gets hurt. "Ms Gloria," and, just like that, Gloria is back to her normal, flamboyant self.

"Oh, hey, Constable Copper Top," she drawls, strutting over and leaning into Eli's side, one thick arm draped over his shoulders with a tinkle of jewelry. Eli is very much aware that he's being used as a deterrent. "This asshole thinks it's okay to creep on women." Gloria gestures at the orange man who's obviously had too much to drink and gone a few too many rounds with the spray tan.

"Fuck you, bitch!" he slurs.

"You couldn't afford me, honey," she claps back, the gathering crowd cheering her on. What Eli wouldn't give for one shift where he isn't on Gloria Hole duty.

Shrugging Gloria's jangly arm off his shoulders he steps up to the swaying drunk, keeping one hand on his baton should this go sideways. "How much have you had to drink, sir?" The man tilts his head to the side, contemplating the question with great effort.

"Suck my cock," is the answer he gives at long last.

"Have you taken any drugs?" From this distance he can't tell with any clarity past the man's alcohol-glazed eyes, but he wouldn't be surprised if there's some sort of unpleasant cocktail in there. There usually is with people like these.

"Fuck you, pig." Sometimes Eli wonders why he chose to become a police constable, why he made the choice to put up with drunks wearing too many layers of spray tan and clothes that don't fit, when he'd like nothing more than to drown them for the sake of evolution and mankind.

"Oh, now you've done it, ho!" Gloria calls out from behind him in a startlingly deep voice, "I'm gonna put my foot so far up your ass you'll be coughing glitter and shitting sequins for a month!"

In any other situation Eli would have laughed at Gloria's creative threat, but now all it does is annoy him and set this relatively mild situation on its way to becoming a fistfight if he can't stop it first.

This is going to be a long shift.

2

THE NEXT TIME ELI SEES GLORIA, SHE'S WALKING ALONG THE pavement, handing out fliers and posing with tourists while looking like she fell into a box of Christmas cheer and decided to wear it; amazingly enough, she pulls it off, candy-cane-striped heels and all.

Even though he has no reason to, Eli pauses by the curb, curious as to what she might be like without a nearby conflict. For a little while he just watches her work. It's interesting seeing this side when he's become so used to drunkenness and rage.

She's strutting back and forth, using the pavement as a stage. He suspects she might have worn that outfit so she'd be difficult to ignore, not that she needs it. Gloria in any situation is difficult to ignore; she exudes a magnetic aura and you just can't help but be intrigued by the contrast of soft features and hard muscle. That and she's at least six foot nine in those shoes.

Eli unfortunately waits until he starts feeling like a creep before approaching, thinking that maybe lurking wasn't a great idea. He could lie and claim she's a suspicious individual, but so far she's done nothing untoward. She breaks into a smile when she finally sees him, waving cheerfully, the bells on her skirt jangling with every move. "Merry Christmas, Copper Top!" she calls out and Eli can't keep himself from a smile at the queen's unending energy.

"Aren't you cold?" he asks, ambling over. She must be, surely.

"A queen never gets cold, honey. Besides, I'm wearing enough padding to be bulletproof," she says in conspiratorial whisper, punctuated by a sly wink.

"Let's not find out."

She barks a laugh, pushing one of her colorful fliers into his hands. "Come see my show and I'll let you check, PC Walsh." Long nails click against his name tag, a plump bottom lip teased with a pink tongue. Eli thinks maybe he should leave. "It's for charity."

"So you do know my actual name?" Charity or no, he's fairly

certain Gloria could convince him to hand over all his worldly possessions if she keeps looking at him like that. When did her eyes get so deep? Maybe they've always been that way and he's just noticing it now she's sober, for once.

He's nearly forgotten the flier, the paper now slightly crumpled from where he's clutched it too hard. It is for charity, Gloria and a few other queens trying to raise money for an LGBTQ+ help center in Hackney. It would be rude not to come when he's been so politely invited, wouldn't it?

"Careful, I might take you up on that." What the hell is he doing? Flirting with a drag queen he's arrested on an almost weekly basis since moving here five months ago? Surely he's violating at least one work ethic?

"I was hoping you would, I'd even let you cuff me if you'd like," she leers, raking his body with heavily made-up eyes.

"You mean you won't resist when I arrest you?" Not that she has before, either, in fact she's been a mostly well-behaved prisoner except for that one time she was sick in the back of his patrol car.

Gloria laughs, her bells jingling along in an oddball cacophony reminiscent of Santa Claus, if he just so happened to be a man in drag. Eli can't keep the smile to himself. He'll have to go see the show now or face a pout for the ages the next time he's called in to arrest her.

He'd hate to disappoint.

3

THE SHOW IS AS CAMPY AND OVER THE TOP AS ELI THOUGHT IT WOULD be, but also a lot better than he expected; Gloria is shining in her role as host and comedian, the entire room drowning in laughter when she presents each act. She has talent, he'll give her that. By the end of it she has the audience in the palm of her hand, despite insulting every last one of them, and Eli suspects she's earned a few extra donations.

Seeing her in her element, it's truly easy to see how much she loves her job, her entire face lighting up when she gets a positive reaction, and she stands out for it. The other queens are all talented performers, too, the burlesque act making him happy he chose to sit at the back of the room since his dignity would likely have been compromised had he been ringside. He's also immensely grateful Gloria hadn't been part of that act or he would have been forced to watch the undressing of that thick, sculpted body; he doubts he would have been able to walk away from that.

At the end of the show the queens disperse through the club to collect any donations and Eli silently prays he isn't in Gloria's section of the room. As luck would have it, he is. Or maybe she just saw him in the audience and decided to claim him for herself. The first sign of her presence are the blood red nails that scratch lightly against the side of his neck, soon followed by warm breath brushing over his ear. "Good evening, Constable." Her flirtatious greeting blocks out all sound for just that moment and Eli is sure her husky voice is going to follow him into his dreams.

He replies in kind and hopes that will be it, but Gloria keeps surprising by slinking around his chair and gingerly perching on his lap. She's fucking heavy, he notes, strapped with muscle under that elegant dress.

"Did you enjoy the show?" She's even more stunning up close

in her red and black color scheme, looking like Morticia Addams decided it was time for something new.

"Very much so." Eli smiles up at her, resisting the impulse to put his hands on her cinched waist, instead reaching into his breast pocket to fish out the twenty he'd stuffed in there earlier for a taxi home. When he goes to put it in her little collection box she tuts and holds it out of his reach, leaning forward to present her artificial cleavage until her massive chest is a few inches from his face.

Deciding to indulge her, he folds the note into a neat rectangle and slips it into her padded bra, never once breaking eye contact. She smirks, ruby lips looking so inviting. Surely she knows what she's doing to him, how tempting she looks; like a seductress tailored with Eli in mind. Impossible to resist.

He's definitely breaking at least one rule, has to be – and he needs to stop trying to break more, he thinks, when he lets Gloria lead him backstage after the queens give one last bow. The hidden corners of a drag club are certainly more interesting than anywhere else he's had the privilege to see behind the curtain, there's no lack of glitter and stray feathers, one lone assistant trying valiantly to sweep it all up while the rest of Gloria's troupe totter around in their six-inch pumps. A chorus of whistles follow them into what must be Gloria's dressing room.

If he thought the hallway was bombarded in drag elements, this dressing room is buried under an avalanche, every available surface covered in makeup supplies and fabric of all colors. The two queens crowding one of the mirrors take one look at them before filing out of the room to a soundtrack of raucous laughter. Gloria pays them no mind, kicking the door closed behind them.

Once more Eli wonders if he might have made a mistake by letting Gloria lead him back here. She's certainly not shy, backing him into the wall, hooded eyes looking deep into his soul.

Eli offers no protest when she runs her fingers down his cheek, slipping her hand around to cup the back of his neck as she leans closer, barely a hair's breadth away, pausing to ask permission. Eli closes the short distance in a heartbeat, sucking on her full bottom lip and inviting her into his mouth with a hungry kiss. If they're going to do this, they'll do it right. There's no going back now.

She tastes like a cocktail, something strong and fruity and he can't help thinking how fitting that is. It's intoxicating, helping him let go of his apprehensions in favor of just enjoying this for what it is. He can't even remember the last time he got laid, much less with someone as gorgeous as Gloria. A part of him whispers in the back of his mind that this will turn into more than just a quick fuck; he's not even sure if he'd mind that.

There's barely any discussion involved before she sinks onto her knees, just a brief: "I'm too padded to get my dick out," offered as an explanation while she pulls down his fly. It's a strange thing to hear from someone looking like she does at the moment. A small measure of guilt settles in his gut, thinking it unfair that he'll get off and she won't, still, she knew that and dragged him back here anyway.

"Rain check?" Eli offers, ignoring the implication he'd someday see Gloria out of drag, he can't even begin to imagine what she'd be like. Probably loud and brash, a rugby player maybe, or a gym rat. He has a clear image of a buzz-cut and a trackie, it's absurd, but he wouldn't be surprised if that's what she looks like.

She only smiles devilishly before wrapping those ruby lips around his cock and sucking at the head, flicking her tongue over the slit. Her talented mouth has him wondering how many men she's pulled into hidden corners like this and why she chose him. He's hardly anything special to look at with his narrow frame and ghostly-pale skin, the curse of being ginger, he supposes. Gloria must be used to so much better.

When she swallows him down he immediately forgets about his self-consciousness; the world narrowing to just the two of them, tucked away in a cramped dressing room with barely any privacy. Adrenaline pumps through his system; knowing the chances of someone listening in are high is turning him on, speeding him along to his conclusion.

Gloria groans as he comes, throat constricting around him, milking him dry until his knees are shaking. He might need to sit down after this. It doesn't even cross his mind to be embarrassed at how quickly he finished when she pulls him into another hungry kiss, biting and sucking his lips.

Later he returns home, dazed and a little confused, stumbling into his bathroom to start the shower. Undressing he's left staring at the smudge of red lipstick on his cock, stark evidence of what he let happen tonight. The memory of Gloria's voice floats by, "I'll hold you to that rain check, Copper Top."

He's in deep now.

4

ELI TRIES TO PUT THE INCIDENT AT THE CLUB BEHIND HIM AND IT works remarkably well. He's nervous when he gets the usual Gloria call, but it dissipates when she turns out to be so drunk she's barely coherent; by the time he's holding her wig back while she heaves into a rubbish bin, it feels just about normal. He thinks nothing more of it as he leaves her in the drunk tank to sleep it off; by his next shift she's long gone and he doesn't suspect he'll see her again for about a week.

That is, until he's walking into the station, nursing his second cup of coffee from the shop down the street and minding his own business when suddenly a voice calls out, "Hey, Constable Copper Top." The voice in question belongs to a beast of a man talking to Cassie by reception, he's tall, broad, and strikingly handsome, if unconventionally so. Eli hates him almost immediately, there's only one person he'll tolerate calling him that name.

"Excuse me?" Eli snaps, glaring at Cassie, who's trying and failing to hide her mirth, it must be her who's informed others of Gloria's nickname for him. "PC Yates, I don't much enjoy being talked about behind my back, much less you spreading that dreadful name." He's being harsh, he knows it, but it's also well deserved; Cassie won't listen to much unless you hammer it into her thick skull. The girl is too headstrong for her own good. That and he's dealt with more than enough *'friendly'* teasing inspired by the color of his hair. "You should keep your gossiping nose out of my affairs." Sparing a glance at the man, he's surprised to find him looking like Eli just smacked his mother, a deep sadness in dark eyes that look awfully familiar.

"You hate it when I call you that?" he asks, adding a note of confusion to Eli's anger. "Why didn't you say anything?"

"Sir, I have never met you before in my life." If possible that sadness seems to get deeper, that giant of a man shrinking in on himself under Eli's glare.

"Christ, sorry, Coppe–" he cuts himself off, face shutting down into blank stone, expressive eyes looking wet, before snatching something off the desk and slumping away like a dog with his tail tucked between his legs. Something in Eli's chest twists painfully.

"What the fuck is wrong with you?" Cassie bites out, a fire blazing in her eyes that makes even Eli want to take a step back. "He was going to ask you out, you cunt," she hisses and Eli becomes increasingly confused, feeling like he's missed out on a crucial detail.

Understanding suddenly dawns on Cassie's face, her mouth slipping into a surprised O. "You didn't recognize him, did you?" She's still angry, but it's been turned down to a furrowed brow and flat lips. Eli suspects there's a storm coming if he doesn't apologize to the right people as soon as possible.

"Should I have?" If there's one thing he hates it's feeling insecure, and right now he's feeling like a prize idiot, though he doesn't know why. Then it dawns on him, the thing that had been on the desk, the glittery fabric of the clutch hitting him like stray lightning.

Gloria.

"Oh." He really should apologize, he'd run after her if he didn't know Gloria to be long gone already. How could he not have seen it, how did he miss the queen who's been causing his feelings to rebel for so long, standing right in front of him? He made Gloria cry. Shit. He hadn't even thought that was possible, but Gloria out of drag is clearly a lot different than when she's on stage or starting a fight.

"Yes, oh," Cassie seethes. "You're going to apologize to him or I'll kick your skinny arse." Eli doesn't doubt she would.

"How was I supposed to know?" he defends himself, "I've never seen him out of drag." And that sad, strange man, with his long hair and soft eyes, had not at all been what he'd imagined. It does nothing to lessen Cassie's fury.

"Doesn't give you the right to talk to him like that." She has a fair point, he had been rude, but in his defense he hadn't had all the facts.

"Here," she angrily scribbles down a phone number on a Post-it, putting the name Andrew Everett above it. "You should wait a little while, he won't answer his phone while crying." From the sound of it she knows Andrew quite well. "If you hurt him again, I'll hurt you."

"How exactly do you know him?"

"He's my cousin," is all the explanation he gets, stated in such a way that he feels grateful she even gave him that much.

Taking the note, he enters the number into his phone under the name of Andrew/Gloria so he won't forget, though he doubts he ever could. The image of that beaten down posture forever burned into his mind is so inherently wrong he never wants to see it again. Almost immediately he sends a text.

[12:36] *I'm sorry. – Constable Copper Top*

It's all he can think to say, it's not much, but hopefully Andrew will reply and they can properly talk about it.

There is no immediate response, leading him to believe that Andrew is either mad at him or crying like Cassie said he might be. He really doesn't like how that makes him feel.

All day he steals glances at his phone; even out on patrol he checks every chance he gets, heart sinking lower each time there is no reply, especially when a little 'read' pops up under the text, letting him know his apology isn't welcome. Maybe he should try again, but he can't force Andrew to talk to him if he doesn't want to. It's ridiculous, really, he can wait for hours and hours at a stakeout, staring down a building while the paint dries, but one little reply that he might never get has him fidgeting all day, even after his shift. Never before has he been so anxious over a text and he's not sure if he likes what that's implying.

Then, finally, as he's trying to relax with the latest series on Netflix, his phone chimes.

[22:54] **Andrew/Gloria:** *it's okay*

He doesn't like the sound of that at all.

[22:56] *No, it's not, I was rude which was wrong of me regardless of whether or not I recognised you.*

[22:57] *Cassie gave me your number, I hope you don't mind.*

He waits with bated breath, watching the little ellipses that indicate Andrew is typing.

[23:00] Andrew/Gloria: *I promise I'll stop calling you Copper Top*

[23:01] *I don't mind when it's you. ;)*

He tacks on one of those awful winky emojis and immediately regrets it, he never uses emojis, he's not a child. Not to mention it is inappropriate in the current situation. It's difficult to forget he made Andrew cry, the correlation between him and Gloria seeming more and more like some alternate reality.

[23:02] Andrew/Gloria: *please don't*

That makes him wonder if Gloria is a mask to hide behind, the man wearing her much more susceptible to fears and insecurities.

[23:04] *I yelled at you for it because I didn't know it was you. Please believe me when I say I don't mind. That name is for you, and you alone to call me.*

It's difficult to know if his words are registering like this and he wishes he could have had his first proper conversation with Andrew face to face. Like this, it's too impersonal and difficult to get a good read on the man behind Gloria Hole. He knows he could easily leave it here and walk away, the exit is right there, he can take one amazing blow job and the easy way out, or he can stick around and take a look behind the sequins. He's ninety percent sure he'll like what's there, so why not stay?

Something tells him Andrew might need a friend, if Gloria's weekly habits are anything to go by, the self-destructiveness brought out under the fluorescents over too many nights. How could he not have seen it before? No sane and healthy person drinks like that, it's alcoholism, is what it is.

He takes the plunge when no reply comes forth, a knot of anticipation settles deep in his gut as he waits.

[23:11] *And I believe I owe you. How about dinner and a movie to set the mood?*

[23:15] Andrew/Gloria: *sure*

Eli releases his breath with a mighty whoosh, the knot

unraveling to become butterflies of the kind he hasn't felt since his first boyfriend in secondary school, giddiness lighting him up in little sparks. He has a date.

5

ANDREW DRIVES A MOTORBIKE. IT'S THE FIRST THING ELI NOTICES when he pulls up to the curb. How could he not? That thing is a beast. Maybe he and Gloria aren't so far apart after all, because Gloria wouldn't look out of place on the sleek, black Ducati. However, when the ridiculous, chrome-detailed helmet comes off, he's met with the unmistakable face of Andrew, that oddly charming amalgam of soft and sharp features that make up a beautiful whole. And of course he shakes his long, dark hair out like some bloody shampoo commercial; Eli refuses to admit he's captivated.

"If you're planning on drinking I need you to know I can't drive that." And there he goes, immediately putting his foot in his mouth.

Just like at the station Andrew deflates at the comment, wincing like he's been struck. "Don't worry," he says to the ground, "I've been trying not to as much." Well, that certainly makes him feel less like a bastard. He'd always seen it as an excessive amount of drinking, but somehow never considered it as something the queen might actually be struggling with.

"I apologize, that was uncalled for. If you haven't realized by now that I am not a very nice man, this might not be such a good idea." In case Andrew changes his mind about this, Eli is going to leave the door wide open.

"I think you're nice," Andrew blurts after a beat of silence, a dusting of red blooming across his cheeks. It's cute.

"That makes one of us." This date probably isn't a good idea. What they should be doing is going up to his flat so he can return that blowjob and call it even; what he does is take the few steps down to the curb where Andrew is standing, straddling his beast of a motorbike. "I hope you have another one of those?" Eli taps the smooth dome of the helmet, he'd really rather not crack his skull open on the pavement should this go sideways, he's seen enough of that on duty.

"Uh, right." Andrew fiddles with a clip on the side, eventually managing to fumble loose what must be his spare helmet since it's identical to the one nestled between his thighs. "Here." The helmet is thrust into his hands so abruptly Eli nearly drops it.

It's a little on the snug side, but it isn't like he has any other options so he just tightens the strap under his chin and swings his leg over the back of the bike. "We'll be late for the film," he prompts, winding his arms around Andrew's thick waist.

That delightfully blushing face is soon obscured as Andrew pulls his helmet back on, securing it tightly before starting the engine and peeling away from the curb. Now he can easily see how Gloria was born out of this man, he drives like a maniac, but luckily keeps to the law, which is something Eli hopes he isn't doing just because he has a copper with him. They make it to the cinema with time to spare and Eli wonders why he ever thought they wouldn't, several close calls still fresh in his memory.

Stepping off that infernal machine makes him realize how endlessly grateful he is he's not part of a motorbike unit, he's perfectly happy to patrol on foot, leaving the reckless driving to the petrol heads that infest the department.

"You all right?" A tentative hand comes out to grab his elbow and help steady him, and it makes Eli irrationally mad, the implication he's weak cutting deep even though he knows Andrew doesn't mean any harm.

"You drive like a maniac," he snaps, immediately regretting it when Andrew takes on that scolded puppy look Eli hates causing. At least he hasn't made the boy cry again. Yet. He never should have suggested this date, should have just apologized and left it at that. Now what? "Come on," he sighs, grabbing Andrew's hand to lead him into the cinema. Might as well see this through.

Andrew trails after him with a sullen look that would suggest he's afraid to speak. Eli can't blame him, he hasn't exactly been nice. Guilt nags at him while he pays for tickets to the latest blockbuster they'd both agreed to watch as a middle ground between Andrew's more artsy, romantic leanings and Eli's preference for history and drama.

This film doesn't have much of either, but it shouldn't melt his brain to sit through it. Really, it's the kind of stuff you'd make out to in the back row. He supposes that isn't an option going by the mood.

Andrew can't say he didn't warn him.

At the concession stand he buys them a drink and a tub of popcorn to share before they head inside. That way, should this become more of a disaster and they cut out dinner in the name of self-preservation, they'll at least have had *something*. His guilt worsens when Andrew is clearly scared of helping himself to the greasy snack. On the positive side, his hand is still encased in a warm grip, then the thought occurs to him that Andrew might be scared of letting go, too.

As the opening credits roll Eli's mind struggles once more to make the connection between this man and Gloria Hole. Where does the queen, with all the subtlety of an overloaded lorry, take up residence when she's not prowling the bars? It's mind-boggling to think someone so timid can flip the switch to such a degree.

It takes him nearly shoving the tub of popcorn up that aquiline nose before Andrew starts relaxing little by little, his rigid posture slumping into a seat just this side of too small to fit his massive frame. He looks like a grown man sitting on children's furniture. It's endearing, dare he say it. Neither of them pay much attention to the movie, Andrew being anxious over whatever is bothering him, and Eli trying to think up ways to salvage this awkward mess before it's too late, because, regardless of common sense, he likes Andrew as much, if not more, than Gloria. He can't quite find the logic behind it, but there's no denying the butterflies he felt when Andrew agreed to this, or the little spark of joy he got at seeing Andrew's face again.

Their palms are turning clammy with sweat, making him think he should probably let go, yet that part of his brain set on this gigantic man says not to, since this might be his only chance to hold his hand. If he can't salvage this he might have to request a transfer to avoid the awkwardness of having to arrest his almost-boyfriend nearly every week. He hopes it won't come to that.

Attempt number one to mend the gap he himself made comes in the form of using their clasped hands to pull Andrew's arm over his shoulder in a slight variation of that age-old move. It's cliché and easily brings him back to the secondary school approach to dating and he fully expects Andrew to move away or tell him to stop, that his chance has been lost. It's pleasantly surprising when Andrew shifts closer to more comfortably drape his arm around Eli's shoulders.

One step forward.

He should have known their tentative truce wouldn't last long once they left the darkness of the cinema. One misplaced comment about Andrew's appetite that he should have kept to himself and all his progress was undone, his date shrinking in on himself and looking decidedly teary-eyed.

Two steps back.

Navigating around Andrew is a lot more difficult than Gloria, the queen having several layers of padding and make-up to help thicken her skin; without his armor Andrew is vulnerable to Eli's scathing words in a way his female counterpart never was. If he's to have any hope of this working he'll have to learn how to apply a softer touch, something he's rarely had to do. As it is now, he's left standing on the sidewalk holding both their dinners in takeaway containers and trying to decide if he would be encroaching too much by calling dispatch to get Andrew's address.

How much more damage can he do?

6

STANDING OUTSIDE ANDREW'S HOUSE HE ONLY FEELS A LITTLE GUILTY; he's here to make this right, Eli tells himself. He did a morally grey thing to get here, but it's for a good cause, if a selfish one. The neighborhood is a lot more middle-class than he expected, a two-story Victorian – Eli absolutely refuses to believe it houses only one person – filling the lot where Andrew supposedly lives. Should he hope for parents or roommates? Which is worse?

A petite woman who's too old to be a roommate opens the door and, just to be on the safe side, Eli throws a glance at the drive to make sure Andrew's bike wasn't a figment of his imagination. It's still there, the chrome helmet clipped to the side. "Yes?" The woman, presumably Andrew's mother, raises a brow, her tone of voice reading as *start talking or start walking*. He wouldn't want to disappoint.

"I'm looking for Andrew."

"You're him," she states, putting a fist to her hip and looking like she's seen some shit, radiating the type of energy Americans seem to have an aptitude for. With a son like Andrew, Eli can't blame her. "He's in the guest house." A nod to the left directs him to the paved path that leads around the corner of the house. "If you make him cry again I'll skin you alive. Now go kiss his ass like you ought to."

"Yes. Thoroughly." Eli's back straightens automatically; so much authority coming from such a tiny woman should warrant the respect of anyone who crosses her path. She must really be something to have brought a huge man like Andrew into the world.

"Good, I'll be watching." With that she closes the door in his face.

He likes Andrew's mother, though he suspects she doesn't like him very much. He'll have to tread carefully or risk getting his arse kicked by a woman twice his age and half his size. He doesn't doubt for a second she could.

Following the path leads him past some well-kept flower beds and rose bushes, through a gate and into the back garden where there is indeed a modest guest house. The lights are on, which is a good sign. At least Andrew isn't crying in a corner with the lights off.

His nerves make themselves known when he steps up to the French doors; heavy curtains are drawn, keeping him from seeing inside. It might be an advantage, there's no guarantee Andrew even wants to see him right now. Glancing back at the main house reveals Andrew's mother watching him from a downstairs window, the sight enough to spur him into knocking so she won't come after him with a vengeance.

"Mom, I told you I—" Andrew cuts off mid-sentence when he sees who it is and Eli's heart clenches when he sees the puffy cheeks and red eyes. "Oh," he finishes lamely, anger dissipating like a tap losing all its pressure.

"I might be the last person you want to see right now, and I understand that, but I would at least like to apologize for being a twat." There, he's said it, not the greatest apology, mind, but it's better than nothing at all. "Again," he quickly tacks on when Andrew just stares at him and sniffles a little.

They stand there in silence for a while, the food he brought from the restaurant long cold, carrier bag swinging lazily at his side. "Andrew?" Eli tries again, "Please say something, your mother is watching and it's somewhat frightening." Eli glances back over his shoulder at the woman still watching them from the window, starting to feel like he's under a microscope. He waves, she glares.

"I know." That brings a little smile to Andrew's face, a brief uptick of the lips, gone as soon as it appeared. Hope, is what it is.

And there he goes, stepping aside to let Eli in.

The main room looks like a fabric bomb has gone off and he spies a sewing machine on a desk by the wall, as well as two sewing mannequins wearing half finished outfits. It doesn't surprise him in the slightest that Andrew makes some of his own outfits, his costumes are simply too unique to be found in any shop without a price tag that would make your eyes water.

"I didn't mean to imply you were overweight," he blurts out when he hears the door closing behind him, trapping them together in the sparkly pool house.

"I'm sorry for being so oversensitive," tumbles out of Andrew's mouth at the same time, their words tangling in the air.

Andrew clearly has something to say, so Eli steps down for now, gesturing for him to continue; maybe if they actually talk like the grown-ups they are they'll be able to resolve this. Really, they should have had this conversation first instead of trying to build a relationship on weekly arrests and a rushed blow job.

"You wouldn't know this from looking at Gloria, but I have some pretty bad social anxiety, it's harder to manage when I'm just me," Andrew starts out haltingly, shuffling his feet where he's still standing by the door. "I don't deal with a lot of stuff very well, especially yelling or stuff about how I look 'cause my self image is pretty fucked too." The way he's talking would suggest he goes to therapy or has before, how he sounds like he's repeating a diagnosis in his own way.

"It's part of why I drink too much," he continues. "If I'm drunk it's easier to pretend my brain isn't such a mess all the time." He's gone onto fiddling with a collection of bracelets on his wrist now in favor of shuffling his feet and tugging at the tails of his shirt. It's endearing to watch and makes Eli feel that much worse for hurting his feelings.

"So, yeah, I'm sorry I didn't warn you, you probably expected to go out with Gloria and not this." Gesturing at himself, Andrew finally looks away from his feet, but only to raise his eyes to somewhere in the vicinity of Eli's knees.

"I like both of you, all of you." Eli takes a careful step closer, unsure of Andrew's level of comfort and not wanting to push it. "I think you're very sweet, and Gloria is, well, Gloria." His confidence grows when Andrew huffs a breath in what could be considered amusement and he takes another step closer. "I'd very much like to get to know all of you better if you'd let me."

And then something he didn't think he'd ever see happens;

Andrew blushes to a color akin to a boiled lobster. With the things he's heard the man say as Gloria, he'd bet on needing something so crass it would make the devil light up to coax a blush out of him. Turns out the opposite is what's needed.

"Will you let me try again?" The bag of food crinkles as he sets it on a clear corner of the little dining table. "Whatever you want," he offers, wanting this date to be on Andrew's terms if he agrees.

"I thought you said you were a dick." The comment takes him by surprise, it's exactly the kind of bravado Gloria would boast and not at all what he expected. "Stop being so fucking nice." A toothy smile contradicts the words and Eli feels like maybe they're back on the right path when Andrew finally looks him in the eye.

"You must bring it out in me," Eli says, feeling his own cheeks heat. "I'm afraid our food has gone cold."

"Screw that." With a sudden burst of confidence Andrew is in his face and Eli realizes a fraction later that he's about to be kissed. Close enough to feel hot breath that still smells like buttered popcorn, Andrew pauses. "Is this okay?" he asks, almost as an afterthought.

Not intending to indulge such a useless question, Eli closes the distance in imitation of their first kiss, catching that full bottom lip between his own. Andrew makes a noise that goes straight to Eli's cock; he's pleased to draw such a sound out of Andrew while at the same time wary of his own reaction, not wanting to go too far. Continuing on in the same vein he keeps his hands above Andrew's waist and his tongue out of it, waiting for Andrew to make the next move and set the pace for what he wants.

Andrew makes no move to pull away, snaking his arms around Eli's shoulders and pulling him close enough to make the angle a little awkward. It seems, heels or no heels, that Andrew is still taller than him, tall enough that he has to stretch to keep his neck from being bent at an uncomfortable angle as the kiss goes on.

He's forced to break it before too long, his calves burning with the strain of keeping them level. "Fuck," Andrew breathes, stooping to rest his forehead on Eli's shoulder. "That was a lot better sober." He had been aware Gloria had had at least one drink that night, but now he's worried exactly how big a part alcohol had to play in their encounter. "Don't worry, Copper Top, I'd only had two when I sucked your dick."

The sudden hint of Gloria has him snorting a short laugh into the mess of dark hair resting on his shoulder. "Good."

"Do you–" there's a deep intake of breath that's shortly released in a whoosh, "–wanna stay?" The words rush out, stumbling over each other and leaving Eli to decipher the mumble. He has to take a breath of his own when a second later he realizes Andrew is inviting him to stay the night.

"If you want me to."

"I'd like to cash in my rain check." That has to be the most polite offer of sex Eli has ever received. To think he could have stupidly left this at one fantastic blowjob in a drag club and never bothered to see if it could go anywhere.

Leaning in, Eli puts them cheek to cheek, enjoying the warmth of Andrew's skin, and whispers in his ear, "Then tell me what you'd like." Being seductive isn't really his forte, but the smirk on Andrew's face would suggest his effort isn't a complete failure.

"We could go to bed and make out for three hours, or," he pauses, leaning back to regard Eli with hooded eyes, "you could let me ride you."

"Where's your bedroom?"

Andrew laughs at his eagerness, a deep rumbling thing he wants to hear much more of in the future, walking them backwards through a door and into the cramped bedroom Eli is curious to explore. For now, though, his attention is more on the large bed pushed up against the wall and he turns them around to steer Andrew down onto the rumpled sheets, leaning in to meet him in a kiss.

With this the confidence he sees in Gloria seems to return, Andrew eagerly meeting his every move, sucking on his tongue like a pro while big hands roam across his back. The difference is astounding, it draws him in like a moth to a flame, keeping him on his toes as arousal sparks through him. Giddy with anticipation, Eli snakes his hands under Andrew's shirt to push it up, revealing the broad planes of his chest, muscle firm under his roving hands. Beneath him Andrew whines encouragingly, pushing up against his touch.

"You are bloody gorgeous," Eli growls into Andrew's neck when they part, leaning back to finally strip him of the offending shirt so he can take in the entirety of that massive chest and wonder why on earth Andrew would be sensitive about his body when he looks like this. No matter, Eli will just have to prove to him how beautiful he is.

Starting at the top he nuzzles along Andrew's collarbones, alternating between nipping and kissing the pale skin as he works his way down to his pecs, leaving a trail of pink marks in his wake, blooming flowers on a blank canvas. Taking one nipple into his mouth he sucks on it until it's nice and flushed, switching sides and repeating, smirking at the noises he's coaxing from Andrew as he flicks the little nub with his tongue.

Before long Andrew's nimble fingers are working the buttons on Eli's shirt open, exposing him to the heated air between them. He's reluctant to lean back, but he'd rather have no barriers, so he's all too happy to shed his shirt in favor of feeling Andrew's chest pressed against his.

Eli kisses him a moment longer before pulling back to just admire the man beneath him: the pink flush on his skin; warm, brown eyes turned nearly black; his long hair fanned out on the bed like a halo. "Turn over, I believe I promised your mother that I'd kiss your arse."

Andrew's answering bark of laughter sends a surge of affection through Eli, loving how the entire man seems to light up with his smile. "I have a better idea." With some more giggling and impressive flexibility, the remainder of their clothes find their way to the floor and Eli is met with a firm behind he's seen more times than he can count, but never has it looked so good as when it's straddling his chest.

"I like the way you think." Sparing a brief thought to the strength of his ribcage Eli pinches one of the pale cheeks before him, Andrew humming with approval while he twists his hair into a little bun, securing it with a hair tie from his wrist.

Not wanting to waste any more time, Eli guides Andrew back a few inches finding only one fault with this arrangement, that being he can't see Andrew's face. Next time, if he should be so lucky, he'll have to ask if he can get a repeat performance of the dressing room without the pressure of time. Delectable arse in position, he spreads the cheeks, revealing the dark pink furl that flutters once before he can put his tongue to the sensitive skin, tracing the rim in sloppy circles.

At a firm swipe of his tongue Andrew lets out a guttural moan, pushing ever so slightly back in a request for more, and who's Eli to deny him? Grinning, he presses just past the rim, having to suppress a gasp of his own when the wet heat of Andrew's mouth envelops his cock without warning.

Getting sucked off by Andrew is a different experience from Gloria, gentler and more slow-paced, but just as mindblowing in its intensity. It even leaves him distracted for long enough to coax a demanding noise out of the man above him, accompanied by a wriggle of his hips to remind him of his promise. Chuckling, Eli buries his face back between those cheeks, placing a teasing kiss on Andrew's hole followed by a flick of his tongue. He loves touching Andrew's freckled skin, seeing in him this different sort of beauty.

He's just got back into the swing of things when Andrew pulls off with an obscene pop, whimpering as Eli's tongue pushes into him again, clearly struggling to keep his hips still. It's not until his jaw starts to ache that he tips Andrew off him, remembering what had been suggested earlier.

"Where's your lube?" he asks, looking around the surprisingly tidy room.

"Fuck, uh, somewhere," Andrew groans, springing from the bed to start digging around in his dresser. Working his way down from the top he exclaims a triumphant, "Aha!" when he unearths a brand new bottle from the third drawer.

With a look on his face akin to an excited puppy, Andrew practically throws himself onto the bed, crawling over Eli and pulling him into a deep kiss he's all too happy to return.

Eli breaks the kiss to ask, "Do you have any condoms?" ignoring the fact that his tongue has been in Andrew's arse, so if Andrew has anything he's likely caught it already. He barely resists rolling his eyes when Andrew grunts in the negative, choosing instead to suck a bruise into his neck. "In my wallet." He leaves no room for argument, he won't risk it any further than he already has.

Overacting his displeasure, Andrew rolls off him so Eli can dig up his wallet and extract the single condom that's been living there for way too long. In the short time he's had his back turned Andrew has been busy and generous with the lube it would seem; three fingers deep in his own arse he's smirking devilishly, lust burning in those dark eyes. It's a sight that spurs Eli on, scrambling to make himself comfortable against the headboard and rip open the little foil packet.

He's barely got the condom on before Andrew is climbing into his lap and smearing the excess lube from his fingers over Eli's cock. "All right?" he asks, waiting for permission before seating himself.

Eli is sure all higher brain function ceases the moment Andrew sinks down on him, taking a few seconds to restart, guiding his hands to those thick hips so he can hold him while they both adjust.

"Fuck, that's good." Adjusting his position a little Andrew puts his hands on the headboard, gripping tight to the frame and using it for leverage as he lifts himself. "First time I saw you I wanted you to bend me over the hood of the nearest car and just fuck me right there with everyone watching." The first time they'd met, Gloria had been wasted and picking fights, Eli happening upon her by accident, drawn by the commotion. He's impressed Andrew remembers anything from that night.

"God, I love seeing you in uniform," he continues, sinking back down, picking up a steady rhythm, rocking back and forth in Eli's lap. "You look fucking indecent." Says the man who's entire body he's already seen through different cut-outs and lingerie. Eli decides to keep his mouth shut about that, busying himself by leaning up and sucking on Andrew's neck.

"Can't believe they let you wear that shit every day, should be illegal." The monologue is broken to make way for a moan, Eli grunting in reply. Usually he isn't one for talking during sex, but the way Andrew does it is very earnest and endearing, very him. Not at all like the manufactured filth plucked out of porn.

"I want to fuck you wearing your hat and nothing else." A twist of his hips just so and Andrew has him gasping, bucking up to meet him in every thrust, moving the pace from eager to near desperate. "Touch me," he breathes. "Please."

Eli isn't going to deny him. Letting go of Andrew's hips he slides one arm around his waist, the other finding its way to the rock hard cock bouncing in time with their thrusts, leaving smears of precome every time it grazes their stomachs. Typically he finds pride in precision, but today he couldn't care less, between the taste of Andrew's skin, the tight heat of his arse, and the silky feel of him in his grip, he's too close to losing it already.

Andrew gives little warning past the tensing of his body before he's spilling over Eli's hand, twitching in his grasp and moaning loud enough that Eli worries for the neighbors. Still he keeps going, grinding their hips together until Eli is sinking his teeth into the meat of his shoulder, panting through his own orgasm.

In the aftermath they slump together, catching their breaths while the sweat dries. "Fuck, that was perfect, thank you," is mumbled into his shoulder where a mass of black hair is resting and all he can do is laugh, petting Andrew before tipping them to the side so they can lay more comfortably. "Next time bring your cuffs."

Now that it's over, Eli's need for order sets in and has him hauling his content body out of the bed, venturing into the adjoining bathroom where he disposes of the condom and locates a flannel to clean them off. He takes care of himself by the sink, returning to the bed where Andrew is sprawled out just how he left him. Still trying to make up for being an asshole, Eli gently wipes the man down, starting at the come smeared on his chest while Andrew sighs sleepily, prompting him to place a kiss on those pouty lips.

"Are you all right?"

"Fucking fantastic, now stop fussing and get in here." Hearing that brings Eli a relief he hadn't realized he needed, his mind subconsciously believing that Andrew's invitation only extended to sex.

Throwing the flannel in the hamper, Eli gladly follows the order, taking a moment to just admire the amazing man stretched out before him, showing no shame in the body he seems to dislike. Wanting to make a point of it, Eli makes sure to touch as much of his lover as possible while he makes himself comfortable, snuggling up to Andrew's side and tangling their legs together. Those fantastic pecs make good pillows, he's quick to discover, pressing his cheek to the sweat-tacky skin.

Falling asleep like this doesn't take long, the sound of Andrew's steady breathing luring him into that comforting darkness with little effort.

Waking up is a different experience. He's so used to sleeping alone that it takes Eli a moment to quell the instant panic when he realizes he's not. Andrew is unfazed next to him, snoring softly on his back. It's…a vision. The drag queen would not be considered a graceful sleeper, jaw slack, creases from the pillow having made a fading pattern on his cheek, and…*is that drool?*

His decision to wake Andrew is not based solely on the thunderous snore that suddenly emerges amongst the softer ones, but more on the fact that he'd rather not be the only one awake should, god forbid, Andrew's mother come calling. A solid smack to the chest has him up in no time. Perhaps it's a little too much, going by the way Andrew shoots up like a loaded spring, coughing and hacking at the abrupt awakening.

Turning to look at Eli he's a little wild in the eye, a look residing there that allows him to practically read Andrew's mind before he's uttered a single word. "What the fuck, Eli?" he squeaks, still coughing intermittently and rubbing at his chest.

"You were snoring."

Andrew flounders, gesturing erratically as if to repeat his previous sentiment.

Eli can't keep the smile off his face any longer, letting it peek forth in a quirk of his lips and a huffed breath. "No wonder you live in the guest house," he quips, referring to the godawful noise that had emerged from deep within that broad chest.

"Fuck you, man," Andrew sighs, falling back down to the bed with a smile of his own. "That was so uncalled for."

"I'll buy you some of those anti-snore strips so you won't frighten my neighbors."

Andrew gives him another withering look before a light goes on in his head and the puppy dog eyes come forth, big and glittering. "You want me to come over?" Honestly, Eli thought that would have been obvious by now.

"Would you like an engraved invitation?" Eli inquires with a fond look.

"I just, I've never really dated anyone before," the words fall out in a jumble, "I mean, I had a friend with benefits once, but that's like, it," he goes on, big hands fiddling with the sheets where they're still pooled over his lap. "Dating a drag queen is complicated." It sounds like the words are being repeated, that someone has rejected Andrew at some point and it made an impact.

"So is dating a police constable." Eli figures Andrew won't want pity or reassurances that this will be easy as pie. "I guess we'll just see what happens."

Next to him Andrew lights up again, rolling his massive body onto Eli, who just groans. When Andrew kisses him, however, he can't find all that much to complain about.

"Are you hungry?" Andrew asks suddenly, pulling back from the kiss to stare down at him. "Mom makes the best breakfast."

Eli has to fight hard not to groan at the mention of Andrew's mother while naked in bed with her son, ignoring the fact that he himself is guilty of the same crime. Surely having breakfast at her table would be the most awkward meal in history, but something tells him Andrew isn't about to let him escape without meeting his parents. "I could eat."

The smile that lights up Andrew's face is worth the coming awkwardness. "I'll text Mom to let her know you're staying."

The view he gets as Andrew climbs out of bed isn't exactly demotivating either; he loves that firm behind *au natural*, no extravagant outfits needed.

"Do you have any tips to gain her approval?" Eli calls after him, sitting up to try and shake off the last dregs of sleep and rub the crust from his eyes. He needs to be as ready as possible before they leave this guest house; today is the day he learns what it's like to be on the other side of an interrogation.

"Nope, she's pretty mad at you for making me cry." Andrew is clearly trying to make light of it, Eli just feels worse for it. "You should have seen her last night before you showed up."

"I'm mad at myself."

"It's fine, you warned me you were an asshole." Andrew appears back in the doorway wearing a peacock-like robe Eli can only assume belongs to Gloria. He looks beautiful.

Finally rising from the bed Eli goes to wrap his arms around his brand new boyfriend. "Don't apologize for me, let's just see if we can make this work before anything else." Someone has to be the one to say it; it's a sad thought, but it's the truth. There's no guarantee this relationship is going to stand up against the pressures of their jobs.

7

Which is why, when he finds Andrew waiting at the station later that day, he assumes the worst. Adding to that, he isn't even in drag which only makes Eli more worried. Still, just looking at him, Andrew doesn't seem to be guilty of anything, he's waiting patiently and throwing pity glances at the junkie nearly slumped in half a bit further down the row of chairs. The rest of the waiting area commotion doesn't seem to bother him in the slightest.

"What did you do, love?" Eli asks, forgetting all about the paperwork he was on his way to file in favor of his possibly-under-arrest boyfriend.

"Nothing, I swear." Andrew is looking at him with those big doe eyes and Eli wonders how anyone could think this man guilty of anything. If he didn't know better he'd be in that group. "I just wondered if you wanted to go eat something since we didn't get to last night." And, Eli hopes, to make up for the most awkward breakfast of his life.

Normally you don't meet your boyfriend's parents on the first date, much less during breakfast the morning after. In contrast to his grumbling mother, Andrew's father had possessed no shame or decorum when it came down to embarrassing his son and being inappropriately proud that he "got some." *Americans*. Eli can still feel the secondhand embarrassment burning as he thinks about it. No wonder Andrew lives in the guest house.

"I'd like that." So far not one single part of their relationship can be considered normal, maybe this lunch date will be the first. "Just let me file this."

He's made it all of three steps before Andrew calls out: "Hey, Copper Top, nice ass!" Eli can only roll his eyes and keep his smile to himself, continuing on his way down to the archive.

Eli usually eats alone, apart from the rare occasion Detective Morrison is in the area – who despite her terrifying presence, makes for a wonderful conversation partner. She'll have a field day when she finds out he's dating the drag queen he's been complaining about since he arrived in this rainy city. She and Gloria would get along like a house on fire. Eli needs that to never happen. Andrew, on the other hand, would probably join the ranks of those Morrison's made cry in less than five minutes.

Andrew walks next to him, their long strides matched and hands entwined. Above them the sun is shining. No one pays them any mind, despite being an odd couple if there ever was one. A uniformed constable and a towering stack of muscle with long, red, acrylic nails.

The cafe he takes Andrew to is the same one he's been frequenting since his first day at this station. It has a sense of normality compared to most establishments in Soho, the drawback is that it's expensive, which is why he only buys coffee here, apart from the rare occasion. Today is a good day for it, their second attempt at a first date. This time he's keeping his mouth shut about the amount of food Andrew is likely going to order.

Eli reckons they're off to a bad start when Andrew picks a simple salad and that's it. "Aren't you hungry?" he asks carefully – *please don't eat less because of me* – giving Andrew's hand a squeeze.

Andrew shakes his head, Eli sighs; this is a conversation best saved for later. Ordering his own food he makes sure to include the side of chips he doesn't want so he can pretend to be stuffed and give them to Andrew. It's hardly subtle, but it will have to do.

Sitting down to wait for their food leaves an awkward silence, since they barely know each other outside of their jobs. That and Eli hasn't been on a date in years and can't remember what you're supposed to talk about. Last time he'd gone out with the only other openly gay man in his little town just because. It had been a means to an end for both of them, a way to get sexual satisfaction and the occasional free meal. They'd got along well enough, but both of them knew it wasn't going to last, their relationship ending with no hard feelings when Eli moved to London.

Then he met Gloria on his first week and he wasn't sure what to think about anything anymore. At first the drag queen had been a passing fascination with a community he didn't know, then she became an annoyance. Every weekend she'd get clocked for something, her record a mile long before she became Eli's responsibility. That he found her attractive was both a curse and a blessing.

He can still remember every detail of the outfit she wore, he'd be hard pressed to forget. The day they met had also been the day he was treated to that lovely behind in a colorful, corseted number that wouldn't have looked out of place on a Mardi Gras float. Maybe Andrew still has that outfit somewhere and they could act out all the filthy thoughts Eli has had about that day, preferably without the guilt following behind.

"What are you thinking about?" Andrew's smooth baritone pulls Eli out of his fantasies and back to the trendy cafe.

Eli smiles, raking his eyes over the man across from him. "You, specifically that feathery outfit you wore the first time we met."

Andrew blushes, looking down at the table as if to say "Aw shucks." It's awfully cute. "I still have that," he mumbles.

"Didn't you say something about wanting me to bend you over?" This is a safe topic for them, even if they're in public. They can't keep a stable relationship built on lust alone, but it's as good a place to start as any – the rest will follow.

"Fuck, Eli, you're gonna give me a boner if you say things like that," Andrew whispers, looking at him with those big eyes.

"I'm just saying it's not outside the realm of possibility." He wouldn't mind wearing his uniform if it would make Andrew happy. Eli has a lot to make up for, after all, it's the least he can do as he's under no illusion that buying lunch is going to fix all the awful things he's said.

"I'll hold you to that."

Eli is fairly positive a life is saved every time his boyfriend smiles, those cute dimples and bright eyes lighting up the room. He considers saying something, but just smiles back.

Their food arrives, and, as predicted, Andrew ends up eating his chips, sheepishly accepting it when Eli transfers them to his empty salad bowl without a word. It makes Eli feel like he can be a good boyfriend if he tries. "I like that you need to eat more than me," he remarks casually, sneaking one of the chips away from Andrew, he hasn't had any in a long while. They're crunchy and greasy, perfectly soft in the middle.

"Sorry." The mumbled apology makes Eli put out a monumental effort to not roll his eyes.

"Please don't apologize, and please don't go hungry because of a stupid comment I stupidly made without stupidly thinking." Since they're tucked away in a corner Eli figures it's all right to have this conversation. The air needs to be cleared, this isn't something he wants turning sour between them. "Just because I sometimes struggle to eat enough doesn't mean you should limit yourself." It took him a long time to realize that coffee couldn't substitute for food, and he's still working on fixing that.

At Eli's admission Andrew's head snaps up fast enough that his hair comes loose from where he's pushed it back, enveloping his long face in a shroud of black. A big hand cards through it, pushing it into place and revealing the surprised look in Andrew's eyes, "But you're always so perfect? It's scary sometimes how perfect you are."

"Appearances can be deceiving." Eli sips his coffee. "Please don't let it bother you, we all have our issues." And that's the end of that as far as he's concerned, their eating habits can be put aside for now, they shouldn't let that weigh down this time-constricted date; twenty minutes from now he needs to go out on patrol.

Across from him Andrew's massive shoulders release some of the tension they've been holding, his posture blooming outwards with a hint of confidence again. It's exactly what Eli needed to see.

After paying up they step back into the afternoon sun. A lunatic in what looks like a g-string jogs past. Humanity as a whole is insane. Andrew whips out a pair of cat eye sunglasses that wouldn't look out of place in his grandmother's sixty-year-old knick-knack drawer. They suit him. Eli can imagine Andrew snatching them up from one of his cluttered surfaces when he left to come here.

They've barely made it a few steps down the street before his hand is enveloped in Andrew's bigger one. Eli smiles, glad that his boyfriend is gaining courage. It's a far cry from the man who'd been scared to eat popcorn at the movies last night.

Back at the station people stare at them and it irritates Eli. He's never hidden his sexuality as such, but he's never been particularly forward with it either, preferring to keep his personal life separate. But here he is, hand in hand with a man wearing acrylic nails and cat eye sunglasses. You'd have to work hard to misinterpret that.

Cassie smiles at them from the reception desk, giving an enthusiastic thumbs up despite the glare Eli shoots her way. Andrew blushes, his hand coming up to cover the slight smile tugging at his lips. Eli's heart melts just a little bit more. Maybe this is going to be all right after all.

He walks Andrew through the station to his shared desk where he picks up his cap, then down to the parking garage where his car is parked. "This is where we part ways for now, thank you for lunch, love." He's sad that their one successful outing is coming to an end. Until Andrew takes him by surprise.

"Can I suck your dick in the patrol car?" It's another one of the sudden bursts of Gloria that seem to pepper Andrew's more timid personality.

Eli huffs a laugh. "No, there's surveillance here, I'd get fired." The disappointment on Andrew's face is both sad and comical. "But you may kiss me," Eli offers as a compromise. "And someday when we're not on camera I can fuck you in the backseat." He barely has the time to finish his sentence before Andrew is on him, those lips pressing kisses all along his jaw.

Eli makes it a proper kiss, tangling his hands in Andrew's silky hair. It goes on for what might be considered a tad bit too long to be appropriate.

"I fucking love kissing you. You're so hot in your uniform." Eli notes there's a distinct hardness pressing against his belly and a question he should have asked sooner bubbles to the forefront of his mind.

"Andrew, do you have a law enforcement fetish?" The evidence is pretty clear, and he doesn't mind in the slightest.

A bright red, splotchy blush spreads over Andrew's face and down past his collar. He tucks his face against Eli's shoulder. "Maybe, I don't know," he mumbles after a while, a tone of please-don't-hate-me running through it.

"We can explore it if you like?" As long as it's safe, sane, and consensual, he's happy to indulge this.

That gets Andrew's attention, his head snapping back up so they can lock eyes. "Really?" When Eli confirms it, a bright smile breaks out on Andrew's face and Eli could swear the entire parking garage brightens from his boyfriend's sheer joy.

Eli has the distinct feeling he's done the right thing and managed to be good today.

"Why don't you come over tonight and we'll break out the handcuffs?" Now all he has to do is not screw it up the rest of the day.

"Don't say shit like that," Andrew whines, covering his noticeable arousal with one big hand and glancing around nervously.

"And you were the one who wanted to blow me in public." Eli shakes his head fondly, finding his boyfriend's contrasting reactions endearing; he obviously doesn't know how to deal with it when he's not the one being crude.

Stealing one last kiss he turns to open the door of the car. "You know my address. I should be home by eight, provided nothing happens." And with that he leaves Andrew standing there looking like an abandoned housewife whose husband has gone to work without giving her a proper kiss goodbye. In other words, a little frustrated, horny, and sad.

Blessedly, nothing out of the ordinary happens all day, just the regular miscreants and a lot of sitting around when he isn't actively looking for trouble to diffuse. The worst of it is an angry baby boomer who didn't get her way in a restaurant and was causing a big scene; a problem that's usually solved fast enough when the police show up.

By the end of his shift Eli is eager to go home and prepare for Andrew's arrival, tidying his already tidy flat and taking a warm shower to wash off the funk of the day. When the clock ticks towards eight he redresses in full uniform, situating his cap just so until he looks like the picture book example of a Scotland Yard Police Constable, sure to fulfill Andrew Everett's fancy.

He's barely done with his finishing touches before the buzzer sounds and he goes to open the door. He'd been expecting Andrew tonight, but on the other side of his door, wearing a very familiar outfit, is Gloria. She looks like a million bucks and Eli is immediately charmed.

"Good evening, Ms Gloria," he grins, reveling in the way Gloria's dark eyes look him over, white teeth catching a painted bottom lip. "Have you come to turn yourself in?"

"Well, Constable Copper Top, I think I might resist just a little," she purrs, eyeing the cuffs attached to his belt. "Don't be gentle." She slips inside and Eli closes the door behind her, pulling the cuffs out of their pouch with a grin. He reckons they'll be just fine.

About the Author

Bo Starsky is a very gay man living in a very small town by a fjord in Norway.

He is of the opinion that there isn't enough LGBT+ fiction that have happy endings. This is why this book exists, and hopefully what drew you to it.

When not writing Bo spends his days fostering cats and keeping company with his exotic pets, Noodle the parrot and Cannoli the python. Neither of which are helpful to the actually writing part of writing stories as they are too cute to ignore.

Along with writing books, you can find Bo writing fic on Archive of Our Own under the same name.

Get More Great Stories

ImprobablePress.com

From ancient gods rising, to road trips on the trail of cryptids,
from romance to mystery to adventure,
Improbable Press specialises in sharing the voices and tall tales of
women, LGBTQIA+, BIPOC, disabled, and neurodiverse people.

Come along for the ride.

Sign up for our newsletter *Spark* at
improbablepress.com

www.ingramcontent.com/pod-product-compliance
Lightning Source LLC
Chambersburg PA
CBHW022033170626
46808CB00003B/1179